Love *Gradı*

By

Mirella Luciani

SORA Publishing

First published in 2013 by
SORA Publishing,
59 Church Road,
Combe Down,
Bath
Somerset
BA2 5JQ
United Kingdom
Email: SORA.Publishing@gmail.com

ISBN 978-0-9926749-1-5
E-pub: ISBN 978-0-9926749-0-8
Book cover design by Elliot Luciani-Kane
Image by Angie Morgan

Thanks to The Rondo Theatre, Royal Crescent Hotel, The
Hope and Anchor and The Eastern Eye for allowing me to
name check them.

DEDICATION

To my children, Susan and Elliot,
with whom I have experienced
my greatest adventures

When thirty eight year old Carla Sterling decides to go to university, the curriculum turns out to be broader than she expects.

LOVE *GRADUATES* is a romantic comedy that follows Carla Sterling's attempts to create a new life for herself after losing her husband, friends, and home to Chlamydia the gold digger. But will Carla complete her studies and get her dream job as director of The Rondo Theatre? And can she succeed in finding love again?

Carla's story is set in and around the elegant Georgian city of Bath. Bianco's Mangia Bene, the family deli is the constant that is family, loyalty, and unconditional love.

Love *Graduates*

Chapter One

"For those of you getting your A level results today, the best of luck. Here's Duffy with something you'll all be praying for; *Mercy.*"

Carla reached across the dark granite counter and jabbed the silver dial, cutting dead the riff. No reminders were needed that only top grades would be good enough to secure Isabella a place to study English at Oxford. They would know soon enough. *Just keep her calm. The wait will soon be over.* Carla poured freshly brewed coffee into Isabella's cup. Isabella stared silently into the small bowl of muesli and poked the lumpy mixture with her spoon. Richard put his head around the breakfast room door.

"Good luck princess."

Isabella forced a smile. Richard stepped into the room. The well-cut cobalt suit Carla had bought a couple of weeks earlier brought out the blueness of his small, sharp eyes. They were all the brighter against his glowing skin, tanned from networking on the golf course. He looked every inch the corporate lawyer.

"Don't worry. You've got my brains. You'll be fine."

Carla allowed Richard his ego trips. It was part of the package. They were a team. He had the career. She looked after the children, their large house, and attended various company functions. Her easy manner always left a good impression on clients, and more importantly, prospective clients of FalconQueen Solicitors. Richard realised early on in his career that the biggest fees were in the corporate department. That was where you had to be if you wanted to become a mover and a shaker in this prosperous practice in the heart of their small Georgian City. So, initial plans to become a criminal lawyer were soon discarded in favour of the lucrative work brought in by business clients. It was a world that suited the whirlwind she had married, and Carla enjoyed the lifestyle that came with it.

Carla offered Richard her cheek. He pecked her on the side of her face and walked out, forgetting why he had come in. Carla rolled her eyes in Isabella's direction. Isabella managed a smile and shook her head. *At least she doesn't look as though she's about to throw up,* thought Carla.

Richard's head reappeared from behind the door.

"Uh, anyone seen my keys?"

Carla picked them up off the welsh dresser. She dropped them into his outstretched hand.

"There you go."

"Thanks. Bye."

Carla didn't answer. He'd be back in a second. She looked over at her daughter, who suppressed a giggle.

"Wallet?" Richard pleaded. He was running late.

Carla produced the wallet from behind her back. She held it over Richard's outstretched hand. He reached to take it, but she snatched it back, opened it, and took out several notes.

"Thanks." She handed Richard the wallet. Carla allowed Richard his ego trips, as long as he remembered who ran the Sterling family.

"And –"

"Don't forget tonight's charity dinner?" laughed Carla. "Thanks for reminding me."

A loud chirping sound mocked Richard. Richard looked over at Lellow, who was basking in the sunlight, streaming in through the patio doors. The canary stretched her wings and resettled herself on her favourite perch, next to the seed dispenser.

"Oh, shut up!" He left for the office. At least there they knew who was boss.

Isabella giggled and put a large spoonful of muesli into her mouth. Carla winked at her. The sallow, green tinge had lifted from her olive complexion, and the sunlight picked out the warm tones in her long chestnut hair. She closed her large hazel eyes as she sipped from the oversized coffee cup. Twenty years before, Carla had sat at a table in the family Deli quietly sipping a cappuccino, waiting to go and collect *her* A level results. But for her, it had been altogether different. There were other things on her mind that day.

"Result!" Robbie's excitement pierced through the wall as he reached the next level of his driving game.

"I wish I was twelve again," Isabella sighed.

"And he wants to be eighteen, driving real cars."

Before Carla's mind had a chance to ponder which part of her life she would return to if time travel were an option, the doorbell rang. Deep down she knew the answer, and the emotions this stirred were beginning to rumble inside her. Carla snapped into *do you realise how lucky you are?* mode, and opened the door.

"Moment of truth!" Isabella's best friend Nellie bobbed up and down on the spot excitedly. Her short black hair was a sculpted bird's nest.

Clutching his remote control car, Robbie ran past Carla, crossing the narrow road that separated their house from Nellie's. On the drive opposite, Alex and Sam, Nellie's younger twin brothers, were acting out a scene from *Robot Wars* with their cars. Robbie wasted no time joining in.

At the wheel of her four by four, Patricia tooted the horn.

"Won't be a minute," called Carla, taking a deep breath.

It was an inspired move to have their children at the same time. Isabella and Nellie were born within ten days of each other, making Carla and Patricia inseparable. In the early days they had carried their portable pink bundles to N.C.T. coffee mornings- a useful incentive to get dressed and out of the house before lunchtime. At postnatal exercise classes, Isabella and Nellie sat next to each other in their car seats while their mothers puffed through core strengthening moves in an effort to get rid of their jelly bellies. By the time the girls were walking, Carla and Patricia were running the local Mother and Toddler group. When the girls started school it made sense to plan their second child together. Several months later it had come as a shock to Patricia that she would be having her second and third child at the same time. Carla didn't know whether to be envious or relieved.

"Come on Bella," urged Carla.

"The sooner we get this over, the sooner we can crack open –"

But Isabella had already bolted from the breakfast room and into the downstairs cloakroom. There was a loud retching sound.

"- the champagne?" offered Nellie.

*****

Richard ceremoniously lifted the bottle of Billecart-Salmon Rose out of the ice bucket. The Guildhall hummed with the buzz of Bath's chattering classes. Pale faces from the past looked on from the huge portraits that hung around the vast eighteenth century room, seemingly amused that time had apparently stood still.

Accountants, lawyers, local businessmen, shook hands, introduced guests and exchanged business cards. Charity functions were always well attended. The business generated was well worth the price of a table, bland food and expensive wine.

The champagne cork popped. Isabella and Nellie squealed. Six champagne flutes fizzed. Richard, still standing, raised his glass.

"To Isabella and Nellie."

"To Isabella and Nellie," echoed Carla, Patricia and Brian. Brian winked at Nellie. Brian had carved a niche for himself at FalconQueen in the probate department. Luckily the work came to him. People weren't going to stop dying. The other partners saw him as a reliable plodder rather than a go-getter, and that was the way he liked it.

Six flutes clinked.

"Shame you didn't both make it to Oxford." There was more than a hint of smug satisfaction in Richard's voice.

Carla narrowed her round chocolate eyes to a *don't you dare* glare. Richard took the hint. He put the glass to his thin lips and took a sip.

"I'm sure you'll both have a great time," reassured Carla.

The girls nodded, but they weren't so sure. That morning Carla and Patricia had waited anxiously by the school gates while Isabella and Nellie collected their results. Fifteen minutes later they had emerged red eyed and tearful. Carla hadn't prepared herself for this. They were both good students. What could have happened? Through the sobs they learnt that Nellie had just missed getting her Oxford grades. For the first time their lives would be forced in different directions. Patricia had been able to reassure the girls that they would have a great time visiting each other, just as she had done with her school friends when she went to university. Carla could only nod in agreement. She

10

hadn't gone to university. She had planned to, but she hadn't. Suddenly it mattered.

Relaxed by the champagne, Isabella and Nellie, began enthusiastically listing all the things they would need to set up a student home. Carla and Patricia exchanged glances. They swallowed, hard.

"How are you two going to cope without your first born?" asked Brian, reading their minds.

"With Bella leaving home, I thought it might be a good idea to go to university myself." For a split second the energetic chatter that surrounded Carla retreated. The rumbling disquiet inside her had formed itself into a sentence that erupted from her mouth.

"That's a great idea," enthused Patricia.

Richard's dry dismissive laugh cut through the nods of approval.

"What do you want to do that for? What you need is a hobby you can turn into a little business."

"Like making jewellery?" Patricia's green eyes sharpened at Richard belittling her friend.

"Exactly. Something you can sell to your friends," he continued oblivious of the snarl curling Patricia's wide mouth.

Carla felt unexpectedly wounded. Richard hadn't shown any interest in what she wanted. He had flicked her off like a dead fly. She felt herself shrivel inside.

"Pierce has arrived," Brian nodded towards the far end of the room.

A white haired man peered at the seating plan. Next to him stood a dyed blond in her mid thirties. She looked around the room with a rehearsed, self-conscious smile.

"I can't believe she's got her claws into him," hissed Patricia in Carla's ear.

Carla glanced over at the simpering blond. "As long as she's got a man to pick up the tab, she doesn't care whose it is."

11

Carla knew the type. This well to do little city attracted them like wasps to an empty cider glass. *Poor Jean, she's been banished to the used wife back lot.*

Carla shook her head. "Does he really expect us to welcome her with open arms? I've known Jean for nearly twenty years."

An amplified cough cut through the social hum. Everyone turned to look at the M.C., a trim, camp man with shiny black hair. He tapped the microphone for effect.

"Ladies and gentlemen, if I can have your attention. In a few moments we will have the first round of our fabulous charity auction."

Carla looked at Richard and Brian. Good, they were busy checking out the wine list with the waiter, a spotty young man, who was trying to look knowledgeable. She conspiratorially curled her long index finger at Patricia and the girls. They closed in.

"Let's wipe the smile off that thick ankled, Marilyn wannabe," whispered Carla. By the time she had outlined her plan, the M.C. was back at the microphone.

"This year we are raising money for the Intensive Baby Care Unit at the Royal United Hospital."

Polite applause. The M.C. put up his hands as if controlling a presidential rally.

"So dig deep. You never know what you might find. I'm never disappointed."

Over enthusiastic sniggering.

The M.C. indicated to Isabella and Nellie. "Now, if my lovely assistants would like to come and join me?"

"You're on girls," winked Carla. Time to put the plan into action.

"Get the bitch," hissed Patricia, a little too loudly. A few heads turned. She coughed loudly, and pointed at her throat. "Got a glitch. Aahem." She swallowed. "That's better."

Isabella and Nellie teetered towards the M.C. in their high heels. Where had the last eighteen years gone? Carla put away that thought for another time. Donald Pierce was standing next to her.

"Good evening all." He exuded that self-satisfied energy unique to middle-aged men who have traded the old wife in for a new model. He felt thirty years old again. He looked fifty-eight.

Carla glanced up. She put her face into neutral, hoping it wouldn't slip into contempt.

"You've all met Camilla?"

"Of course," gushed Richard. "Take a seat."

Brian nodded politely. Carla and Patricia forced a smile that was on the edge of morphing into a snarl. These subtleties were lost on Camilla who seemed to think this moment called for her best Munroe impression. She managed to look vacantly pleased with herself.

"Sorry, we're late." Donald had a fresh sense of purpose. "I was helping Camilla set up her latest business venture."

Richard nodded approvingly. The Marilyn smile became brighter and wider. The large bosom heaved and the eyes feigned naivety. Carla felt like shoving a saucer of cream under her chin. Donald pulled out a chair for Camilla. Patricia leaned towards Carla.

"Latest business venture. What might that be? A self help manual called *How to get what you want by stealing other people's husbands?*"

The M.C. positioned Isabella and Nellie either side of him. Isabella held a large gold envelope.

"Ladies and gentlemen it's time for our first auction. Get your cheque books ready because the Naked Chef himself is offering a two day cookery course at his flagship Italian restaurant, right here in our fine city." He paused to milk a reaction. The crowd oohed obligingly. Isabella held up the envelope.

"Let's start the bidding at one thousand pounds." An arm went up at the back of the room. "Thank you Madam. Who's going to fight you for two days with a naked chef? Do we have one thousand one hundred?"

Two middle-aged fans battled it out until the bidding reached three thousand pounds. Both were in over their heads. To the relief of her husband, one threw in the towel. The M.C. milked the final dramatic moments.

"Does anyone want to offer three thousand five hundred? I'll throw in a free table to my burlesque night at the Komedia next month." He paused and scanned the audience.

Richard poured pink champagne into Camilla's glass.

"We were just saying, with Bella going to Oxford a little business might be just the thing for Carla. Perhaps you and Carla could -"

Oh no we couldn't. Richard had made it too easy. Operation Camilla took off. Carla kicked Richard sharply in the shin. Richard jumped.

"Ouch!" The champagne he was pouring splashed straight into Camilla's lap.

The cold liquid soaked through Camilla's tight cream dress to her skin. Her arms flew up.

"Oh, oh." Camilla looked at the wet patch covering her groin.

Carla and Patricia gave Nellie a wink. Nellie pointed at Camilla. The M.C. clocked the flapping arms.

"Three thousand five hundred pounds from the enthusiastic lady on my right."

Camilla stood up and tried to dry her dress with a napkin, while Richard apologised, red faced. She began to register that all the eyes in the room were on her. The M.C. continued.

"Going once, going twice. Any more bidders?"

Camilla gave the M.C. a confused look. *Great,* he thought, *the more sloshed they were, the more money they threw around.*

"Congratulations Madam. Two days with the talented Mr. Oliver, and you'll be throwing a fabulous dinner party for your father," he nodded towards Donald, "and your friends."

Patricia choked on her champagne. That topped it. Enthusiastic applause from relieved husbands. Carla sneaked a look at Donald. He looked as though someone had shoved a lemon in his mouth. He'd be picking up the bill. She stifled a laugh as Camilla disappeared in the direction of the ladies toilets.

"The perfect place for someone so full of shit," mouthed Patricia.

The starter was served. Melon and Parma ham. Carla stabbed the melon with her fork and plunged her knife into the firm flesh.

"Mmm, my favourite."

*****

The following afternoon, Carla's family celebrated Isabella's success. Mamma Bianco had made the special cake, normally reserved for Christmas, christenings and First Holy Communions. It sat on the counter of the family deli, Bianco's Mangia Bene, covered in soft white icing, glistening like a full moon. Twelve egg yolks and whites would have been separated, sugar added and the mixture beaten into a creamy giant zabaglione. The whites were whisked into a frothy meringue before the two mixtures were blended together with magic ingredients to create a deep moist sponge, which was then filled with a layer of vanilla and a layer of chocolate cream. As children, Carla and her younger siblings, Gianni and Angela would fight over the saucepans used to prepare the sweet fillings, their spoons duelling as they scraped away every last delicious trace.

Carla was still on a high from the previous evening. The wet patch on Camilla's crotch had got bigger when she tried to wash the stain out of her dress. She had returned to the table holding her tiny silver bag over her groin and insisted

15

Donald take her home, which he did reluctantly. He hadn't finished his meal, and Camilla's cooking wasn't up to his wife's standards. The evening had also cost him a fortune, and he wanted to try and get his moneys worth working the room and making new contacts. Operation Camilla had been successfully completed, and the two families had spent the rest of the night dancing to the music chosen by a middle aged DJ who knew his audience.

Mamma Bianco cut into the moon cake. She splashed each generous slice with Vermouth. Mamma picked up two plates, handed them to Robbie and squeezed his cheek.

"You such a handsome boy. Just like your grandfather, nonno Enzo." She crossed herself.

"Ouch! Nonna!" complained Robbie.

"Go, give the cake to Nina and Gina." She pointed at the table next to the window. Two pensioners talked animatedly, gesticulating wildly. They appeared to arguing but for the bursts of laughter that punctuated their loud exchanges. Robbie groaned, making a mental note drop the plates on their table and run before Nina and Gina could latch themselves onto his cheeks.

"Nonna, this is the best." Isabella licked her spoon.

Then she remembered something, rooted around in her bag, and pulled out a booklet. She pushed it towards Carla.

"What's this?" Carla looked at the cover.

"Patricia dropped this off for you. It's a prospectus for Aquae Sulis University."

Carla glanced at the cover and pushed it away.

"It was just a silly idea. I'd never find the time." Stung by Richard's lack of support on the subject Carla had already decided her place was at home, not studying for a degree. That ship had sailed a long time ago.

Gianni glanced over at the prospectus. His long dark eyebrows rose. He put down the yellow chalk he'd been using to make his elaborate drawings on the specials menu and grabbed the prospectus. Carla and Angela ignored him.

"You should go," encouraged Angela, "I think it's a great idea. You're the one with the brains."

"What about me?" The little boy in Gianni still looked for recognition.

"Your brains are in your hands. Stick to cooking."

"Thanks. And you stick to your boring office job. That's suits you too."

Angela dug her fork into a slice of moist sponge, gave Gianni a sugary smile and promptly jabbed it into his hand.

"Ouch!" He sucked on the non-existent wound. "Watch the hands."

At a small table, Michael Nolan pretended to be engrossed in his book, but Augusto Boal's *Theatre of the Oppressed*, wasn't nearly as entertaining as the family drama playing out at the counter. He got the feeling that the brunette really did to go to university. Something was holding her back. She seemed confident enough, the way she held herself. Slim, but shapely. Nice bum. He closed his book and checked his watch. Three thirty. He was meeting Nathan at the The Rondo Theatre at four. Who would have thought that when Nathan left Edinburgh last summer, they would both end up in the same city? It would be like going back to their uni days. Michael caught sight of his reflection in the mirror. *Maybe not.*

Mamma Bianco placed a large iced tea on the counter.

"The lady over there." She pointed to a woman in her mid thirties with curly golden hair. She sat on her own, and was keeping the toddler at the next table entertained playing peek-a-boo. The toddler gurgled with delight every time the woman's face revealed her wide smile from behind her pale freckled hands.

Carla picked up the iced tea. She caught the woman's eye and smiled at her. The woman fanned herself with a napkin. Her table was in direct sunlight and her fair skin was turning pink. That iced tea would go down well.

Michael slipped his book into a carrier bag. He glanced at the pink-faced woman. A cold beer with his mate would hit the spot. He stood up. His arm hit something cold and hard.

"Aargh!" The icy liquid stung Carla's skin.

Michael turned around. The woman with the nice bum was catching her breath. She clutched a large empty glass, the contents of which now were running down her top and forming a puddle around her expensive looking shoes.

"Oh God! I'm so sorry." Michael grabbed the napkin from his table. "Let me help clean it –uh, you-up." He started pressing the napkin into the dark stain around Carla's stomach. As the eldest of four, cleaning up spillages was a reflex reaction.

For a moment Carla didn't know where she was. An ice cube glided over her bare abdomen. Everything went into slow motion. Carla gulped a couple of mouthfuls of air snapping back into reality. She grabbed the napkin from the offending hand.

"I can manage. Thank-you." She blotted herself with the soggy napkin.

"Please, let me pay for the damage," offered Michael, who realised that every face in the deli was looking on with a mixture of surprise and amusement. His mouth dried. He should have been in the pub having a cool pint with Nathan, not providing afternoon panto for the ladies of Bath.

"It's okay. Really, you've done enough." Carla was surprised at her curtness. Was this some kind of divine retribution for humiliating Camilla? But Camilla had deserved it. Whatever it was she just wanted this man to go away and stop making them the centre of attention.

"Sorry, I was just leaving." Michael picked up his carrier. Just before reaching the door he compounded his humiliation by tripping over a chair leg. Beads of perspiration formed on his temples. *Quick, get out.*

As the door closed behind Michael, Carla let out a sigh of relief. He wouldn't be showing his face at the deli again. *Nice accent though, Irish. Soothing. Unlike the rest of him.* She pulled her wet top away from her skin. An ice cube dropped out and hit the floor.

Michael snatched the cool air that rose up from the weir. The sound of rushing water calmed him. New city, new job, new life. He was a fish out of water, and acting like one. There was a rush of air above him. He looked up past the small stone bridge lined with independent shops selling books, souvenirs, and snacks. Hovering above Pulteney Bridge in the cloudless sky was a red and yellow hot air balloon. *Everything is going to be fine* Michael reassured himself. Catching sight of the clock above the library he saw he was running late, and pulled his phone from his back pocket.

Carla stepped out into the bright sunshine carrying the usual large box of food from Mamma. She had left Isabella and Robbie behind, as they wanted to go shopping in town. Now wearing Gianni's huge Mangia Bene T shirt, she was going straight home to change. Orange was not her colour. Carla walked along the riverbank towards the car park, away from the tourists packing Bath's mini Ponte Vecchio.

As Michael punched in Nathan's number, he was distracted by a cute bottom wiggling towards the car park. He slipped his phone into his shirt pocket and jogged towards the derriere. Before he had time to tell himself he was behaving like an idiot, he was next to Carla and the words tumbled from his mouth.

"Please, let me carry that. It's the least I can do."

"I'm fine." Carla gave the man her politest smile and carried on walking. "My car's two minutes away." She took another self-assured step- straight into a crevice. Carla's foot rocked. Her knee buckled.

"I've got you." Michael held onto to box with one hand and caught her firmly around her waist with the other. Michael lifted the box out of Carla's arms. Reluctantly, she let go of it.

19

"Thanks." *Why am I thanking him? If he hadn't distracted me, I wouldn't have lost my balance in the first place. Just humour him. In a few minutes I'll be in the car, and that will be that.*

The university prospectus sat on the top of the box. Michael remembered the conversation he had overheard in the deli.

"So you're not going to apply?"

"Sorry?" Carla looked at the Irish stranger, puzzled. He looked normal enough. Quite handsome, if she was going to be really objective. Had she missed something?

"Apply for what?" she asked coolly.

Michael looked down at the prospectus as they continued walking.

"University."

First he drenches me in iced tea, then he makes it clear he was listening to a personal conversation. Carla's cheeks prickled as she flushed with a mixture of embarrassment and anger. She stomped to a stop and faced him, aware that her face had turned blotchy and crimson.

"You were eavesdropping," she accused.

"I didn't need to," Michael defended. *What on earth have I said now?*

"Are you're calling my family loud?" Carla's dark arched eyebrows had risen to the middle of her forehead.

"Yes. I mean no." Michael felt he was digging himself into a hole. He knew from experience that women seemed to have a knack of knowing exactly where a conversation was going, like a predator leading its prey in for the kill.

"So what are you saying?"

Michael's mind went blank. He caught sight of the prospectus and tried to get back on track.

"Just that if you want to go to university, it's not too late," he suggested as gently as he knew how. He didn't want to set her off again.

"What makes you think I want to go?"

"Well, you wouldn't be so defensive for a start."

Carla's mouth dropped open. *The cheek of the man.* Michael saw the fiery indignation in Carla's eyes.

"W-what I meant was, it might seem daunting go back to studying at ... um-"

"My age?"

"As a mature student." *What's she getting so tetchy about her about?* At forty seven, he had to have ten years on her. Michael proceeded with caution. "What I'm trying to say is, sometimes it's good to step out of your comfort zone. It can help you ... find out who you are."

"I - I." Carla grabbed the box. "I don't need any lectures from you, thank you. I know exactly who I am. Who do you think you are?"

Carla strode away, head high, trying to look like a thirty eight year old grown up who had all the answers, but a shadow passed over her heart. Crack! Carla's right heel rocked sideways. Great! She took off her shoe. The snapped heel was hanging like a broken bone. She threw the shoe in the box and limped the last few metres to her car.

*****

By ten the next morning Carla was pushing a shopping trolley holding a bright orange toaster and kettle. Isabella pulled out the packets of duvet covers from a shelf. Her long slim nose wrinkled with dissatisfaction.

Carla pretended to look through the bedding on the adjoining shelf, but her mind was elsewhere. Did she really know who she was? By the time she was twenty she was married with a baby. She hadn't planned it that way. All her friends had gone to university. Suddenly there had been no one left to sunbath in the park with, no one to talk to about boys, and no one to ask which colour she should buy that top in. When her two closest friends came back from University that first Christmas they had already moved in with their undergraduate boyfriends. To them, Bath was

21

suddenly the most boring place on Earth, and they couldn't wait to get back to London, which they did, straight after Christmas. To be fair, they had invited Carla to celebrate New Years Eve with them, but Carla's mother needed her, so she stayed put. Then, one snowy January day Richard walked into the deli, a shower of snowflakes clinging to his thick floppy brown hair. He ordered a lasagne. Carla watched him out of the corner of her eye while she pretended to rearrange the array of coffee beans and teas on the shelf behind the counter. He was obviously enjoying every mouthful, closing his eyes and making a spontaneous "mmmm" sound every time he swallowed. Richard made a fuss of Mamma Bianco, telling her what a great cook she was. He proved his point by coming in every day for the next two weeks. His easy charm and healthy appetite won Mamma over, and she would dish him up even larger portions than the hearty offerings she already offered her customers. By the time he asked Carla if she would like to go to the cinema, to see the latest *Die Hard* film, Carla and Mamma knew that Richard was twenty-five, a newly qualified solicitor with one of the largest firms in Bath, and an only child with no surviving parents.

By Easter Carla and Richard were officially going out. She was the envy of her university friends, who complained about their skint, smelly, unromantic student boyfriends. It was her turn to feel grown up and interesting.

One sultry Sunday afternoon the following August, Richard arrived to pick Carla up. Mamma handed him a hamper and winked. Richard tapped his nose, suggesting a conspiracy between them. They were up to something. Carla was sure of it.

"So where are you taking me?" she ventured.

"Donald and Jean are having a garden party. It'll be deadly, but I can't say no to the senior partner. If I want to be a partner by the time I'm thirty he's the man who can make it happen. Your mother has packed some goodies to keep him sweet."

Carla laughed. Food, no, great food was her mother's answer to everything. Maybe she was right.

They drove down the steep windy roads that separated Bath from Bradford on Avon, then through the medieval streets that gave the town its nickname, Little Italy. Richard turned into the small car park near the canal towpath.

"You never said Donald lived on a boat?" joked Carla, puzzled.

"He doesn't" laughed Richard. "I wanted to surprise you. We're having a picnic by the river. Just us."

"That's very romantic of you." Carla meant it. Richard was very good at making the smallest moments feel exciting. She put her hand on his thigh and squeezed it appreciatively.

Carla savoured the last spoonful of her mother's creamy tiramisu. The delicious blend of cognac and coffee lingered in her mouth. She lay on her back and looked up at the cloudless sky. It had been the darkest of winters, but thanks to Richard the light had come back into her life.

"Glass of champagne?" Richard stroked her silky hair.

"Mmm. You've thought of everything," Carla purred. She closed her eyes. For a moment she thought of her impending reunion with her old school friends. Anna and Sara were back in Bath the following day. They had ditched their boyfriends at the start of the summer and had gone off to climb Machu Picchu. Carla looked forward to hearing about their adventures. But it also reminded her, that she too had once made adventurous plans, plans she hadn't given a second thought to since the day Richard and his floppy hair had walked into the deli.

Pop!

"Keep your eyes closed," ordered Richard mysteriously.

Carla squeezed her eyes tightly shut and clenched her fists with excitement. She listened to the champagne fizz into the glasses. Then nothing.

"You can open your eyes now." Richard was leaning over her holding a champagne flute full of dancing bubbles. There was something sitting at the bottom of the flute. Carla focused. Bobbing gently at the bottom of the glass was a dainty ring with a small cluster of diamonds.

"Carla Bianco, will you marry me?"

Carla held up a quilt cover in neutral colours. She'd been staring through it for several minutes.

"That'll go with everything," she offered, trying to sound enthusiastic.

"Too ordinary," chirped Isabella, excited at the prospect of going off to university and living the life of a real student.

"Sounds like my life. And when you're gone ..." Carla's voice trailed off. It wasn't fair to make Isabella feel guilty about getting on with her life.

"Mum, what's the matter? You've been quiet all morning."

Carla plonked herself on a double bed. A shop assistant busily dusting a display of bedside lamps frowned at her. Isabella sat next to Carla putting her hand gently on her shoulder.

"I don't know," she lied to herself.

"You do mum. What is it?"

"I'm beginning to feel like I've missed out – on something I meant to do." Sharing her feelings with Isabella wasn't easy. It made Carla feel like the child, when she'd always been the one encouraging, consoling and praising her daughter throughout her childhood. "I was only going to take a year out to help out at the deli before going to university. Then I met your father ..."

"Thank God for that," laughed Isabella, "for a minute I thought you were going to tell me you were having an affair."

"What?"

"Sorry. All through sixth form someone's mother or father seemed to get caught having an affair. Must be that middle age crisis thing you're all going through."

"Thanks, but last I heard George Clooney was still in Hollywood."

"There's always Johnny Depp. Doesn't he have a house in the Circus?"

"Not my type. Too broody. I prefer a simple man." Carla giggled forgetting she was in miserable mode.

"Like Dad you mean?"

They burst out laughing and rolled back onto the bed. The shop assistant glared at them.

Isabella caught her breath and took her mother's hand.

"Do it. Go to university."

"What makes you think they'll want me?" Carla lacked the self-belief of youth.

Isabella pulled herself upright and fumbled inside her bag.

"There's only one way to find out." Isabella waved her mobile.

It was time to stop feeling hard done by. Carla sat up and took the phone.

*****

Chapter Two

A week later Carla knocked on the open door marked Department of English and Drama. She was ten minutes early for her 11 o' clock appointment. A sparrow like woman with a neat grey bob peered over her computer screen. Carla stepped tentatively into the small office.

"I'm Carla Sterling. I have an appointment with …" Carla checked the letter she was clutching.

"Professor Nolan." The bobbed sparrow smiled kindly. "Yes, Professor Nolan has had to go to a meeting with the Dean."

"Oh."

"He's arranged for his colleague, Dr Bolton to see you. Take a seat." She pointed a bony finger at a couple of chairs next to the drinks machine outside her office. "I'll take you through shortly."

Carla took a seat. Apart from the few posters advertising local theatrical and musical events, the foyer was bare and eerily quiet. She tried to imagine what it would look like filled with students chatting and moving in different directions through the four or five doors around the perimeter. But she couldn't see herself amongst them, part of it all. The urge to make her excuses and leave began to take a hold. As if reading her thoughts the sparrow reappeared.

Carla sat opposite Dr. Bolton, a curvy woman in her early forties, with wild auburn hair. Dr. Bolton scrutinized the exam certificates and scant C.V. Carla had sent in. Carla bit the inside of her bottom lip nervously.

"Your A level results are very good."

Carla released her bottom lip.

"But they do go back twenty years. Have you done any relevant reading since?"

Carla had done a lot of irrelevant reading. The first ten years reading *Cosmopolitan* had given her a PHD in the art of the blowjob. During the next ten, she had matured into *Good Housekeeping*, which had done nothing to turn her into a domestic goddess. But she'd fooled Richard, and that was good enough. Carla had always been far more interested helping her children research their school projects and lending a hand with the school plays. During nativity preparations, Isabella had nominated herself the leader of the three kings. While handing over her gold parcel, Joseph had let out an enormous fart. Isabella deftly diverted the attention from the red faced little boy by announcing "I bring you gold and some medicine for Jesus' bottom burps."

Carla smiled at the memory. "I've helped out with all my daughter's school plays and I've read all the plays and books she's studied."

"Any particular favourites?"

"Uh ... To be honest I just love reading. Was this a trick question? Bernard Shaw ..." she ventured.

"Why?" pressed Dr Bolton.

He makes me laugh Carla wanted to say. *Think. Why does he make me laugh?*

"I like the way he criticises society and makes the audience laugh at the same time." Carla held her breath. Right answer?

"Yes, *Pygmalion* being a good example. And you're ready to undergo a transformation of your own?" Dr Bolton's pale green eyes suddenly seemed uncomfortably penetrating.

"Er ... I've not thought about it like that, but ... yes."

"You do understand the level of commitment that will be expected from you?" The green lasers searched Carla's face. "Despite what you may read in the media about what students get up to, it's a challenging three years."

"Dr. Bolton, I realise it's been twenty years since I left school, and that I'll have to work hard. My grades may be out of date but they are good. I've waited a long time for this," asserted Carla, surprising herself. "I want to do this and I will be committed."

A flicker of sympathy crossed Dr. Bolton's face.

"It's not that simple I'm afraid. This course is very popular. We're already full for this year."

"Sorry? I don't understand. Why am I here?" Carla's surge of confidence drained as quickly as it had risen.

"We wanted to see if you would be a suitable candidate for the course, and you are," reassured Dr Bolton, "but you would have to apply through the proper channels to start next year."

"I see." Carla stood up. "Thank you."

She shook Dr Bolton's hand, covering her disappointment with a forced smile. Carla didn't want to wait until next year. The last time she had waited until next year, she had woken up twenty years later and didn't recognise herself.

The corridor passed her in a blur. Maybe she should just forget about trying to make up for what she didn't do twenty years ago and just get on with her life, the life she had now. Behind her, Professor Michael Nolan entered the far end of the corridor. He stepped into Dr Bolton's room.

"Sorry I landed you with that interview. How did it go?"

"If it's alright with you I'd like to put her top of our waiting list." Dr Bolton knew that the presence of one or two conscientious older students was the perfect wake up call for some of the less mature undergraduates, some of whom believed getting a degree was simply a matter of turning up for a few lectures, in between parties, alcohol and sex.

The sunlight stung Carla's eyes. She slipped on her Channel sunglasses, a birthday present from Richard. At thirty-eight, she was a grown up, getting on with her grown up life. Time to put the past behind her.

*****

"Is that idiot husband of yours over his midlife crisis?" Patricia gave Jean Pearce a hug.

"Glad to see Donald has come to his senses," echoed Carla giving Jean an affectionate kiss on the cheek.

The past few weeks had flown by. The summer holidays had come and gone and the rhythm of Carla's life was once

28

more dictated by Robbie's school run. She helped out at the deli a couple of lunch times a week, and thankfully there were no further collisions with nosey customers offering unsolicited life coaching. Isabella had finally found a quilt cover she liked; a purple, and black ethnic affair that she felt reflected her new status as an undergraduate. It was only a couple of weeks before she left for Oxford. Everything was as it should be, well at least according to the fifth of Deepak Chopra's Seven Spiritual Laws of Success. Isabella had given Carla the book the day after her interview with Dr Bolton. But, try as she might, *stepping into the field of all possibilities* was proving tricky. Her life felt more like *The Trueman Show*, a series of loops following a tired familiar pattern. Today's loop had taken her to Queen Square for the annual Boules Festival.

"It was his prostrate that did it," said Jean matter of factly.

The women were distracted by a cheer from the FalconQueen team. Richard's boule had stopped just in front of the jack, taking the match from their opponents. The defeat wiped the perfect bleached smiles from the faces of the city dentists.

"His prostrate?" Carla was intrigued.

"He was worried he wouldn't be able to keep the minx happy. I couldn't care less if he never got it up again. Once you hit the menopause, gardening is a much more attractive option."

Carla and Patricia burst out laughing at Jean's sanguine attitude. Good for her.

"I bet the madam already has her sights set on her next meal ticket." Patricia nodded in the direction of the boules pitch opposite. Camilla stood holding a glass of white wine, pretending to take an interest in the game between a team of accountants and some beefy rugby players.

29

Carla's phone rang. She fished it out of her clutch bag. It wasn't a number she recognised.

"Carla Sterling speaking," she said in her stern you'd better not be a cold caller voice.

"Hello, Carla, it's Charlotte Bolton."

Carla blanked.

"From the drama department at Aquae Sulis University. One of our prospective students has deferred for a year. We'd like to offer you his place. Can you start next week?"

"Next week?" spluttered Carla "Eer, Yes. Thank you."

"Excellent. I'll be in touch."

"What?" enquired Patricia. Carla looked as though she had been hit on the head with a mallet.

"That was the university. I-I start next week."

"Congratulations." Patricia threw her arms around Carla.

"Make the most of it," smiled Jean. "I spent one of the best summers of my life locked away in a cottage in Devon with my food technology lecturer."

Carla and Patricia tried not to make eye contact as they supressed the images forming in their heads. They whisked a couple of glasses from a passing tray and took a large gulp.

" I'll bet he had no trouble getting his soufflés to rise." quipped Patricia.

Jean looked straight at her, a wicked twinkle in her eye.

"*Her* soufflés were as light as air."

Carla choked mid swallow. Patricia's eye widened with admiration. *Bet Donald wasn't privy to that episode in Jean's life.* Her eyes widened further as she glanced over in Camilla's direction. Camilla was chatting to Richard and Brian with that innocent doe eyed look she affected whenever a pair of testicles was within a metre radius. Camilla giggled at something Brian said and stroked his arm. Patricia pursed her lips. No way was her husband going to be Camilla's next meal ticket.

"That's one soufflé that is about to be well and truly deflated." She strode over in Camilla's direction.

Jean nodded approvingly. Carla looked on in amusement. She was buzzing from Dr Bolton's phone call, and Camilla's predictable stunts were becoming boring. There was only one niggle to deal with now. How to tell Richard.

*****

Carla picked up her fringed shoulder bag. She looked for approval at Isabella, who was still in her oversized pink pyjamas. Carla was wearing her new black cargo trousers, a plum cap sleeved T shirt and a fitted cropped denim jacket. She hoped it would give her a studenty edge without seeming to try too hard.

"Trendy and ready for uni. You look great mum. You'll fit right in," Isabella reassured her mother.

"Apart from the wrinkles."

"You haven't got any. Now get going."

Carla opened the front door. Patricia was at the wheel of her black beast. The twins were pushing and shoving each other to get in first.

"Robbie," called Carla "Hurry up. Patricia's ready to go."

Robbie ran down the stairs, toothpaste clinging to the corners of his mouth. He headed for the door. Carla took his school bag off the peg next to the door.

"You might need this." Carla was used to being her son's short-term memory.

"Oh, I forgot." He grabbed the bag and dashed over to Patricia's car.

"That'll be the inscription on your gravestone," laughed Carla.

Patricia waved and mouthed "good luck." Carla blew her a kiss. Butterflies were gathering in the pit of her stomach. It was her first day at university, twenty years later than planned. She would be happy just to blend in.

"Go, or you'll be late," ordered Isabella.

"All right, Miss Bossy. I'm going."

Carla fought her way through the school traffic. When she reached the edge of the city, the congested roads gave way to open countryside. The trees were already developing a red tinge. It seemed odd, that around her everything was starting to die when she felt she was starting to live. Richard had been surprisingly relaxed about the whole university thing. Apart from making a sarcastic joke about choosing something more practical, like accountancy, he had accepted Carla's decision to take the place on the drama course. The drive through the countryside was barely five minutes, but most of the routes in and out of Bath meant negotiating one of the seven hills surrounding the city. Carla took the steep descent towards the roundabout. Normally she would have gone straight over it on one of her girlie shopping trips to Bristol with Patricia. Today, she turned left past the only building, a country pub. Carla slowed right down and read the sign on the wall; *Aquae Sulis University*. She smiled to herself. It had taken twenty years but she was here, and that was all that mattered. The butterflies in her stomach did a dervish dance. She took a deep breath and drove through the gaping wrought iron gates, joining a queue that snaked along the narrow road towards the campus.

The car park was already heaving. Carla managed to find a space at the back. Car doors opened. Large numbers of young adults, who reminded her of Isabella and the numerous school friends who randomly appeared in her house, clambered out. There were a lot of short skirts, quirky hats, and brightly coloured hair. The young women looked confident and carefree. Nothing like Carla. Suddenly she felt like an outsider. Her excitement turned to fear. Why would these bright young things want anything to do with her? They had left home to get away from middle-aged housewives like her. Head down, Carla made her way to the block where Charlotte Bolton had interviewed her. Carla chided herself. Dr Bolton had placed her trust in her. She could have offered the place to someone else, but she offered it to her. *So stop whinging.*

Carla lifted her eyes from the floor. A few students were already waiting in the corridor outside the lecture hall. A couple of them looked pale and dishevelled, as if they'd just picked themselves up of someone's floor and dragged themselves in. Carla fiddled nervously with her hair and pretended to focus on the notice board. A man in his early seventies shuffled towards her supported by a walking stick. She smiled at him, reassured that she wouldn't be the oldest student there after all. You really were never too old to learn, and at least she had a good chance of making it to the end of the course alive. The folder the elderly man carried slipped from his hand. Carla rushed to pick it up.

"Thank you, young lady."

"Pleasure." She handed him the folder. It felt good to be called young. Probably needed his eyes checked.

"A mature student?" The voice now betrayed an innate grumpiness.

No, he had twenty-twenty vision. "Yes. I thought I'd be the oldest here. Are you looking forward to ..."

"... teaching us, Dean?" The voice cut in from nowhere. It belonged to woman with a halo of strawberry blond curls. She looked vaguely familiar.

"Thankfully, I've plenty of staff for that. Can't abide today's undergraduates. In the sixties we were out to change the world. Nowadays they all want to be famous. Frankly they'd be better off doing a proper job, like plumbing." The Dean shuffled off towards the lecture hall muttering. "You can't get a plumber for love nor money these days."

"That makes me feel so much better about being here." Carla smiled weakly at the angel who had saved her from further embarrassment.

"Don't mind him," laughed the woman, crinkling her small freckled nose. "He looks well past retirement."

The penny dropped. The deli. That was where Carla had seen her. Never knew what she wanted. Scatty but pleasant.

"We've met before," ventured Carla. "Bianco's Mangia Bene?"

"Of course." The angel chuckled. "You've dried off."

"Oh God! The iced tea incident. Don't remind me."

"I thought he was rather handsome. Was he brave enough to show his face again?"

"No, thank goodness."

The doors opened and the students filed into the lecture hall. A hum of excitement filled the air. Carla and her fellow mature student followed the flow of bodies.

"I'm Jenny."

"Carla."

The women sat together. The seats either side of them remained empty as the bright young things stuck together in tight little groups.

"I have to admit, it's a relief to see another mature student," said Jenny, reading Carla's mind. "It's a bit scary being surrounded by all these fresh faces." A look that said she'd put her foot in it came over her pixyish face. "Sorry, no offense, I didn't mean … you have a really nice face …"

Carla laughed. "None taken. I'm glad there's someone here who doesn't think I've got the plague." She nodded to the ring of empty seats around them.

The Dean stood, stooping over his walking stick at the front of the room. He was wearing his professional benign face. Nothing like the grumpy old man in the corridor a few minutes earlier. He cleared his throat.

"Welcome" he said, sounding like he meant it. "I would like to start by introducing you to the members of the faculty who will have the pleasure of teaching you this semester, starting with the latest addition to our team, Professor Michael Nolan."

Professor Michael Nolan stood up and walked towards the Dean. Carla's mouth opened and closed like a goldfish. She was looking at iced tea man. Jenny nudged Carla.

Forty-five minutes later the students meandered out of the lecture hall.

"I can't wait to get started now," said Jenny excitedly.

Carla was not so sure. She'd been rude to *Professor Michael Nolan*. Now she realised why he'd encouraged her not to dismiss the idea of starting a degree. It was his job. He was just being helpful, and he sounded perfectly normal, up there, addressing everyone. *Maybe he won't recognise me,* she reassured herself.

"You decided to give it a try?" The voice was soft and honeyed.

Carla jumped. The professor was standing next to her. She looked up at him and squirmed. "Er, yes ... I did. I-I must apologise, I was very rude when ..."

"When I practically drowned you in iced tea. Perfectly understandable," he burred gallantly.

Jenny stood behind the professor and gave Carla a wink.

"Well, I look forward to seeing you in class." Michael made his way to the small group of lecturers answering the concerns of individual students. Carla looked at Jenny and smiled.

"Might be a good idea to put your tongue back in."

"Lucky you. He's gorgeous."

"He was being polite. Anyway, I've come here to learn. I'm married, happily married." Carla wiggled her ring finger to make the point. "And so are you it seems," she said teasingly, looking at the delicate gold band on Jenny's left hand.

Jenny's face fell. The light went out of her eyes. It was a look Carla had seen before, many years ago.

"I was."

"Were?" asked Carla gently.

Jenny's eyes filled with tears. "He died."

"I'm so sorry." Carla was stunned. She squeezed Jenny's hand, conscious that she didn't want to pry.

"Brain tumour. Last year," Jenny volunteered.

A tear dropped onto the back of Carla's hand.

"I'm just a cliché really," Jenny continued, as if to herself. "Coming here, looking for a way to rebuild a life of some kind."

"I'm glad you did. It's a new beginning, for both of us." Carla looked around the empty lecture hall. It didn't matter that she wasn't going to blend in here. She was twenty years older than the other students. Nothing was going to change that, but every night she had her family to go home to. That was her life, the life she wanted.

*****

"Are you sure that's everything Bella?" Carla tucked the orange kettle and matching toaster beside a pillow on the back seat of Richard's BMW. She looked at Richard through window of the study. He was still on the phone giving instructions to his secretary. It was the same when they went on holiday. He'd be 'busy' with work until it was time to set off, then he'd grill Carla over the packing.

"I can't go without Mister Bluey." Isabella dashed into the house to fetch her favourite cuddly toy; a small pale blue rabbit which had guarded her against night monsters since she was three.

After their introductory talk in the lecture hall the day before, Carla and Jenny had gone in search of the refectory. They had found a small table next to the glass wall overlooking the adjacent field, and filled each other in on their lives thus far. Jenny had been due to start the course the year before. Then Martin got the devastating news. He had been given just a few months to live. They had wanted children, but for no apparent reason Jenny hadn't become pregnant. Professor Bolton had arranged for Jenny to defer until the following year. Jenny had spent months sleep walking through her days. It was only when Charlotte Bolton had rung her to remind her that the place was waiting for her that she felt she was waking up and becoming present again. Jenny didn't want to spend another year living a half-life. Martin wasn't coming back. She had to do something to try and re-join the world.

Guilt jabbed at Carla's heart. She had everything Jenny wanted, so she played down her life. She moaned that Richard was always working, that Isabella would soon be gone, and that Robbie struggled at school because of his dyslexia. Then she felt shallow for complaining. So, it was a relief when the conversation turned to the semester's reading list and they had set off in search of the campus bookshop.

Isabella appeared clutching Mister Bluey. Carla saw Isabella as her three-year old self, griping her monster repeller. She promised herself she wouldn't cry when they left her at the halls of residence at Oxford University. Isabella got into the back of Richard's BMW. It was his pride and joy, a Five Series with pale leather seats. Carla suspected he begrudged the few occasions it was used as a family car, and attracted the usual debris of crisp packets, drink cans, and sandwich wrappers. Robbie had already made himself comfortable. He was wrapped like a papoose in Isabella's quilt, his fingers busy at the Game Boy. He had his father's floppy brown hair, although Richard's was beginning to thin at the crown. A sore point. Carla hoped Robbie would take after Gianni who had a thick thatch, which he proudly ran his hands through whenever Richard boasted about the minor celebrities he played golf with.

Carla peered through the study window. Richard was still talking on the phone, nodding and laughing. Carla caught his eye and pointed at her watch. He raised his index finger. One more minute. Carla glared at him. What he was doing was always ten times more important than anything else. *Sod it*. She needed to pee.

Richard was at the wheel. His Oakley shades made him feel cool. The engine purred. Carla got in the passenger seat.

"Thought you were ready," he quipped.

Carla thumped him.

Five hours later Isabella's room in the halls of residence had undergone a colourful transformation. It resembled something out of The Arabian Nights, with Mister Bluey surrounded by sequined, beaded and batiked cushions clustered on the single bed. During lunch at a country pub, Carla had picked at her food. She would miss having another female around the house to counteract the testosterone her men released into the atmosphere.

It was time to leave Isabella to her new life and return to Bath. Richard looked up at the grand architecture of this city of spires.

"The first Sterling to go to Oxford," he said, chuffed.

"Why didn't you go to Oxford Dad?" asked Isabella.

Richard looked at his feet, anticipating his family's response.

"Didn't quite make the grades."

"Dunce!" Robbie pointed at Richard. Out came the expected bursts of laughter. Robbie poked Isabella in the ribs. "Keener!"

Isabella reached out to grab him, but he swerved out of reach and took off along the path. She raced after him, caught him and covered his head in kisses.

"Gerroff," he protested waving his arms around, pretending to push her away.

Carla smiled at the familiar scene. Soon they would leave Isabella behind and life would never be the same again. *Damn!* She'd promised herself she wouldn't cry.

*****

Chapter Three

'Home in a couple of weeks. Can't wait. If I find Robbie's been anywhere near my room, he's dead. Love Bella xxx.'

Carla laughed and closed the text. As soon as they had returned from Oxford, Robbie had tried to commandeer her room. He had complained it wasn't fair that he was the only one who didn't have a double bed. So much for brotherly love.

Carla had been surprised how quickly she adapted to Isabella's departure. Busy with reading lists, and running Robbie to tennis, football, and swimming, there was little time to brood. Richard was often late home from work, and Carla was as grateful as ever that Mamma Bianco would hand her a bowl of something delicious to take home for supper. Last night it had been gnocchi, drenched in simple tomato and basil sauce. It hadn't suffered too much from being reheated at ten-thirty, the time Richard had finally got home. Then he just picked at it telling Carla he's grabbed a snack earlier. Carla said nothing. She was relieved she hadn't put in the time to prepare it, leaving her free finish reading Arthur Miller's, *All My Sons.* It appeared to completely slip Richard's mind that Carla was at university. Life for him went on as normal, but Carla felt she was living a double life: mature student by day, 1950s housewife-imposter by night. Still, all she had to do was get through the next two weeks to make it to the Christmas break.

*****

Michael Nolan leaned on the lectern. The shadows under his eyes darkened under the florescent lights. In two weeks he'd be on a plane back to Dublin, but not before marking a pile of essays, most of which would be mediocre, and some completely incompetent. Even fewer would combine thorough research with critical analysis and individual flair, and remind him why he loved his job.

"You're all aware that your first essay, on Arthur Miller, is due in on Monday. I'm sure you'll all give one of the great dramatists of the twentieth century the time and attention he deserves."

Jenny grimaced. Carla mirrored her look.

"I don't want to play this game any more," said Jenny in her little girl voice.

"Well, you have to," mimicked Carla.

A couple of the students glanced at them, wondering what the two older ladies were up to now. Carla and Jenny would frequently collapse into laughing fits. The last one was when Jenny had tried to coax some escaped sheep back through the gap in the fence. The sheep responded to their inexperienced shepherd by running off in the opposite direction, where the Dean was shuffling towards his office. One of the sheep had skimmed his shins nearly taking him off his feet. He shook his stick frantically at the women who, like a pair of naughty schoolgirls, had run off to hid.

Carla glanced towards the lectern. Michael was surrounded by a small group of anxious students with last minute questions about their essays.

"Like bees around a honey pot," observed Jenny.

"Does that include the boys?"

"Especially the boys."

"You don't think …?"

"Why should you care, Mrs Smug Married?"

"No reason."

"If you say so. Now, library or coffee?"

"What do you think?"

Carla and Jenny left Michael to his fans, and power walked through the biting easterly wind to the refectory in a block close by.

"Damn those Russians." Jenny covered her face with her scarf.

"What have the Russians ever done to you?"

"They should keep their wind to themselves. It's bloody freezing."

They broke into an unaccustomed jog, and lunged at the refectory door. At that moment the door opened. They flew through it. Jenny's foot landed heavily on a skateboard, whose owner was in the toilet. She took off, arms flapping.

"Aaarrghh …"

Carla chased after her. She grabbed the back of Jenny's coat and pulled. With a thud Carla landed on her back with Jenny on top of her, limbs thrashing like a dying fly. To their horror they looked up at a walking stick and a pair of legs in brown tweed trousers. The Dean glared down at them, shook his head and shuffled towards a table where Charlotte Bolton stifled a laugh. Carla felt a blast of cold air hit the back of her neck.

"Bloody Russians."

*****

The heating hummed quietly. Carla's books were arranged in a semicircle on the dining room table. Inside the semicircle, on a pristine A4 pad Carla had written "Why Joe Keller, in *All My Sons* is a good example of the 'protagonist' in a dramatic tragedy." She flicked straight to the index at the back of a book the size of a brick. A collection of quotes would be a good start.

"Mmm ... tragic nature ... recognizable suburban types." She made a note and smiled to herself, recalling the dramatic entrance into the refectory earlier that day. They had tucked themselves away at a table in a corner. Ten minutes later, the pointing and sniggering had stopped, and Carla and Jenny had relaxed into a cosy chat about Carla's plans for a Christmas gathering at home.

"I thought you two would be busy in the library." The women jumped. Michael stood in front of them, with a tray holding a large bowl of steaming soup, and a teasing smile in his eyes.

"I need to defrost my brain first," chirped Jenny.

Carla kept quiet. After their disastrous first encounter she'd been determined to keep a low profile where Michael was concerned.

"Mind how you go." Michael chuckled as he walked away.

Jenny raised her eyebrows. "News travels fast."

Carla groaned.

Richard hovered at the dining room door. Carla glanced up. His legs looked particularly muscular in his new squash gear.

"See you later."

"Can you pick Robbie up after squash?" Carla had spent the afternoon doing the supermarket shop and running Robbie around. She wanted some uninterrupted essay writing time.

"I can't. You'll have to do it." Richard's voice was matter of fact. His commitments were important.

"You've hardly seen him all week. He keeps asking when you're going to watch him play football. All the other dads do."

"I can't tonight."

"Just pick him up after your game. For God's sake Richard, you were the one who encouraged him to go in the first place."

"I'm busy after."

Frustration and anger rose through Carla's body. She squeezed the pen between her fingers.

"Really, and how busy would you be if he was one of the star players?"

"I'm meeting Adam Peters." Richard's voice was annoyingly calm and reasonable. "He's an important prospective client. You'll meet him tomorrow, at the rugby."

Crap! Carla had completely forgotten. "The rugby? I've got an essay to write."

"For Christ's sake Carla, I'm trying to get ahead in the firm. How the hell am I going to get dinosaurs like Pierce out of the way if my own wife doesn't support me?"

"And what about you supporting me?" Carla's hands grips the arms of the chair.

"I do. Every day I go out to work and support you. But why would you notice? Every time I look at you, you've got your head stuck in a book."

Before Carla had time to launch a counter attack, Richard was out the door, slamming it behind him.

"Fine," she said to the walls. "Leave it all to me, for a change."

*****

Robbie snuggled deeper under his duvet. His prize collection a model cars, a Jaguar XKR, an Aston Martin Vanquish and his favourite Ferraris lined the shelf above his bed. Carla sat on the bed reading *Harry Potter*.

After Richard had stormed out Carla had struggled to get into her essay. In between loading the washing machine and unloading the dishwasher she managed an introduction on how Joe Keller in *All My Sons*, fulfilled Aristotle's definition of a tragic protagonist. Just as she settled into explaining how Joe Keller's son Chris presented the audience with an opposing belief system, Carla realised she was already ten minutes late picking up Robbie. She grabbed her keys and flew out of the house.

When she arrived at the sports centre Robbie was helping the young coach tidy up. Everyone else had gone. The coach lapped up Carla's apologies, taking the opportunity to squeeze her arm. She was near the top of his list of MILF's and took pleasure in her gratitude. Robbie didn't like the way his coach looked at his mother and dragged her away complaining he was hungry.

Carla closed the book on a dramatic cliff-hanger.

"Oh, mum. You always finish on the best bits."

"You're lucky I'm still reading to you at all," she laughed. "You'll be growing a beard soon."

Robbie rubbed his cheek, unenthused by the thought.

"I thought dad was picking me up tonight."

Carla sensed Robbie's disappointment. "He really wanted to," she lied, "but he had an important meeting."

"I didn't score any goals anyway. Dad used to score lots of goals."

"Well he doesn't any more. Anyway, I bet Dad can't make model cars as well as you can, and you're a much better skier. Look what happened when he tried to copy your jump at the end of that black run."

Robbie chuckled. "At least he got a ride in the helicopter ambulance."

Carla kissed the top of Robbie's head and got up. "Night sausage."

"Night, night mum."

She closed the door behind her.

"Mum?"

Carla popped her head round the door.

"Promise me you won't tell anyone you still read to me."

"I promise. Now go to sleep."

Robbie turned on his side and curled up into a ball.

Carla tossed and turned. She had managed to add a couple more paragraphs to her essay, but it took her forever to decide what she wanted to say and how she wanted to say it. Reading plays was one thing, writing about them was so much harder. It was like asking her brain to perform like an Olympian after twenty years as a couch potato. Exhausting. Now, running over her fight with Richard in her head, she couldn't get to sleep. And where the hell was he? It was well after midnight.

A key turned in the lock. Silent footsteps stopped outside the bedroom. The door opened slowly. Richard slid out of his clothes and slipped under the duvet. He put his hand on Carla's face. She opened her eyes.

"Sorry." He kissed her on the forehead. She smelt alcohol on his breath.

"No, you're right," she whispered, "I should support you. The essay can wait."

"Thanks." Richard turned over.

Carla cuddled into his back. She snuggled her nose into the back of Richard's neck and breathed deeply.

"You smell different."

"Probably that cheap shower gel in the showers at the squash club," mumbled Richard. "Night."

Carla rolled onto her back. *Cheap.*

*****

From the FalconQueen rugby box, Carla cheered and berated in the right places, a fraction of a second behind Patricia, who followed every move on the pitch with an understanding that equalled Carla's confusion. The teams were neck a neck with just couple of minutes till the end of

45

the match. That much she understood. But, after a fitful night's sleep, she just wanted to do her bit and go home. Adam Peters, lucrative potential client, sat the other side of Carla. Down to earth and unassuming, Adam had inherited a small but very profitable engineering business from his father. His success was due to luck rather than enterprise and he wore it lightly.

"Richard's a formidable squash player," he said to Carla watching the home team struggle for possession of the ball. "We had quite a game."

"And quite a night," responded Carla trying to sound casual. She blamed Adam for keeping Richard out late and disrupting her sleep.

"But in bed by eleven."

Carla dropped her guard. "Eleven?" She was as puzzled as she sounded.

"I know. I'm a light weight. The kids get me up at six."

Carla nodded. Why had Richard come home so late? She looked past Patricia to where Richard and Brian were chatting with a couple of established clients; a woman in her fifties who ran a successful publishing business specialising in children's books, and a younger man who designed office spaces. Richard was a master at giving people his complete attention, making them feel special. That's what must have happened last night. Bath was such a small place. It was impossible to go anywhere without bumping into someone you knew.

"Champagne?" Camilla held a small tray between Carla and Patricia.

"Latest business venture?" Patricia took a glass.

"Just helping out a friend. Never know who you might meet here."

A groan rose from the crowd. The away team had scored.

"Bugger!" Patricia turned her attention back to the pitch.

Camilla leaned towards Carla.

"Playing away makes victory all the sweeter. Don't you think?"

Carla felt unexpectedly unsettled. She caught the scent of Channel. They were wearing the same perfume.

"Champagne?" purred Camilla.

*****

Carla added her name to the already long list of essays offered up for marking. She looked forlornly at the pathetic couple of pages she had placed into a cardboard box marked "Year 1 Theatre Studies Essay."

Sunday morning, after the rugby match, Carla had woken up feeling nauseous. Within half an hour she'd been floored by a migraine. The day passed her by as she drifted in and out of sleep until the nausea, headache and dizziness subsided later that evening. It had left her feeling weak, drained, and fit for nothing. *Hell!* She should never have accepted that glass of champagne.

Jenny signed the form and placed a thick pile of paper in the cardboard box.

"Thank God that's in. A whole weekend holed up with no one to talk to. It's enough to drive you insane."

Carla sighed. "Sounds like heaven."

*****

A week later Carla stood in the corridor outside Michael's office waiting for Jenny to come out with her freshly marked essay. That week Carla had made a note of all points she would have made in her essay if it hadn't been for that stupid row with Richard, the boring rugby match, and the migraine brought on by Camilla's poisonous

47

champagne. Now Carla's stomach was in knots waiting to face Michael.

The office door opened. Jenny waved her essay in the air and beamed. There was a large sixty eight percent ringed in red on the front page. Carla forced a smile, wishing she could feel more magnanimous towards her friend.

"Well done. You deserve it." At least she meant it.

"See you in the library, no make it the refectory. Time for a large piece of lemon drizzle." Jenny floated down the corridor.

Carla's feet dragged like a couple of lead weights into Michael's office. Michael looked away from his computer and gestured for her to sit down. He tapped at the keyboard for a few seconds. It felt like a lot longer. Carla clenched her hands nervously. Finally he took a deep breath and faced her.

"I'm sorry. I didn't get time to finish it," she lunged in, reading the disappointment on his face. "Every time I sat down to write, I was interrupted."

Michael picked up the two flimsy pages.

"Carla, what little you've written shows potential, but you're not doing yourself justice. And if you give in to distractions, you'll fail the course."

Carla felt thirty-eight going on thirteen. Tears fought to erupt. She swallowed hard in and effort to push them back.

"Maybe I've made a mistake, thinking I can cope with a family and studying." Carla stared at a paper clip on the dark blue carpet.

Michael's eyes softened. "Aren't you enjoying the course?"

"I love it." Carla's voice cracked. "I'm learning so much. I've found the part of me that I'd lost when I-," she paused, surprised at her own response, "stopped being Carla Bianco." *Keep swallowing, don't cry.*

Michael paused for a moment. "This will have to be second marked next week, so just this once, I'm going to give you extra time to finish it."

"Th-thanks". Carla was taken by surprise. "I won't let you down."

Michael handed her the essay. "Don't let yourself down Carla."

*****

Carla sipped her tea. Her books were laid out neatly on the dining room table. Michael was right. She was always running around after everyone else. She was entitled to some time for herself. Determined to make the most of the two hours of peace before Robbie was back from school, Carla set to work. She picked up her pen and mouthed as she wrote, "Joe Keller initially refuses to see beyond duty to his family." Her mobile rang. Carla picked it up ready to switch it off. She saw it was her mother's mobile, which meant Mamma wasn't in the deli.

"Mamma, you okay?"

Mamma Bianco's friend Nina was still gabbling as Carla pulled her handbag off the table and ran to the front door.

"Tell her I'm on my way." Carla was already in her car.

Carla spotted Nina and Gina sitting in a corner of the half full Accident and Emergency waiting room of the Royal United Hospital. She rushed towards them. They stood up, jittery with worry.

"What happened?"

"She was okay, having a nice walk," said Nina in her thick Italian accent.

"Then she lose her balance. She say she is dizzy." Gina clutched her chest dramatically.

"Next minute she fall," finished Nina.

Carla ran to the reception desk. The receptionist looked up from her computer screen.

"My mother, Mrs Bianco. She's had a fall. Can I see her?"

A small round nurse put a file on the counter. "I've just seen to Mrs Bianco. You must be ..."

"Her daughter." Carla's heart beat hard. "Can I see her?"

"Of course. Follow me."

"Is she okay?"

Before the nurse had time to answer Carla faced a grumpy Mamma Bianco, coat on, and clutching her handbag.

"I bloody fine. I not dead."

Carla felt a flood of relief through her body.

The nurse suppressed a smile. "We've checked her over. No broken bones. You can take her home."

Stoney faced, Mamma Bianco sat up in her bed.

"Open the curtains. It's too dark."

Carla did as she was told. She knew it wouldn't be easy to keep Mamma Bianco confined to her bed.

Gianni cradled his face in his hand, trying to work out how he was going to look after the deli and Mamma on his own. "What did they say at the hospital?"

"Apparently she's been having dizzy spells for a couple of months now."

Angela gave her mother a stern look. Mamma Bianco raised her eyes to the ceiling, like a belligerent teenager.

"She needs to have some tests done," continued Carla. "The doctor says she has to take things easy while they find out what's wrong."

"Bloody doctor!" Mamma Bianco folded her arms.

"If you don't do as the doctor says I'll get a lock put on this door and make sure you do," scolded Angela.

Gianni was quiet. Quiet meant worried. Carla couldn't stand back and do nothing.

"You can't manage on your own. I'll come in and help you out" she offered.

Gianni lifted his head. "You going to have time?"

"I'll come in on Saturdays," interrupted Angela. "We've got to make sure Mamma gets her rest."

They looked at Mamma. Her eyes were narrowed and her lips pressed tightly together.

"Anybody would think we were plotting to poison her," said Carla.

The siblings burst out laughing. Nina and Gina bustled in. Gina carried a tray with a large bowl of freshly made minestrone soup. There were three large wine glasses on the tray. Nina carried a bottle of Chianti.

"Don't worry," said Nina squeezing Carla's cheek and pushing her out of the way. "We look after your mother."

"And we help with the deli," added Gina.

Mamma clapped her hands approvingly.

Gianni looked up to the heavens. "God help me."

*****

The rest of the week had flown by. In between lectures Carla had dropped in at the deli to take over serving customers so Gianni could get on with preparing food. Nina and Gina had been confined to entertaining Mamma. They had brought along their ancient record collection to play on an old turntable that had belonged to Carla's father. Their favourite was the 1964 Italian Eurovision winner, *Non ho l'etta per amarti* –(Not old enough to love you). The dramatic piano intro swept down the stairs and into deli for the umpteenth time.

"God, they're like a bunch teenagers," moaned Gianni.

"It's parent's revenge," laughed Carla as Gigliola Cinquetti's heart-rending lyrics were drowned out by Mamma and her gang singing their hearts out. "Well at least they've moved on from *Shaddap You Face*. They're probably singing into their hair brushes."

Gianni shook his head. "Let's hope they swallow them."

*****

Carla picked up her pen. Her books were just as she'd left them when Nina called from the hospital. She had two days to finish her essay. With Richard away for the FalconQueen AGM at some windswept hotel in Devon, she could ignore the housework and concentrate on getting her essay finished. Now, Where was she? "Joe Keller's son, Chris, presents the audience with an opposing belief system," Carla mouthed, starting a new paragraph. "Right, find a quote."

Carla turned the pages of the play. She felt pleased with herself. Writing an essay wasn't that big a deal. There was something quite satisfying about getting her thoughts organised on paper when the rest of her life was spent rushing from pillar to post.

Thud! Thud! Thud! Robbie's football pounded against the wall in the hall.

"Robbie, will you stop that, I'm working."

Carla found a quote and started to write.

Thud! Thud! Thud!

"Robbie, did you hear me? Take it outside."

"I'm bored," whined Robbie.

Thud! Thud! Thud!

Carla finished the quote. Right, next point.

Thud! Thud Thud!

Carla slammed the pen down and marched into the hallway. She grabbed the ball.

"For God's sake Robbie." She opened the front door. "Go and play outside." She tossed the ball onto the front lawn.

Robbie dragged his feet in protest, towards the front door. Bored or not Carla didn't care. This was her time. A screech of brakes and Robbie picked his feet up. He ran out onto the lawn. Patricia's car was stopped at the end of Carla's drive. The football lay in the middle of the road. Carla ran out after Robbie.

"Now look what you made me do," she shouted.

Patricia was out of her car. She pulled Carla back. Robbie stood on Patricia's lawn clutching the football about to burst into tears.

"No harm done," Patricia read the stress on Carla's pinched face. "Robbie, go hang out with Alex and Sam." Patricia handed her keys to Alex as he jumped out of the car followed by his twin. The three boys disappeared through Patricia's front door.

"I'm so sorry. You could have been hurt." Carla suddenly felt drained.

"It was just a ball." Patricia looked into Carla's pale face. "What's the matter?"

Carla burst into tears.

Patricia put the mug of tea on a coaster next to Carla's books.

"There you go. Nice and hot with a big dollop of honey. That'll bring the colour back to your cheeks. Carla sat at the table. She wiped her eyes.

"Thanks."

"Listen, I'll keep Robbie overnight. You get on and finish that essay. Now does he have anything to bring in for the cake sale on Monday?"

"I made some rock cakes. Didn't you see them in the kitchen?"

"I thought they were for a ritual stoning. I accidently dropped one and it cracked a tile," laughed Patricia.

Carla managed a smile. "Gianni normally gives me something, but he's run off his feet. I didn't like to ask. They're not that bad, are they?"

"Not if you've got titanium teeth. I'll make an extra batch of cup cakes. He can take those and if you're a very good girl I'll bring you one over."

"With pink icing?"

"Deal."

*****

Michael wrapped up his lecture. "Don't forget to make start on your reading over the holiday. Happy Christmas everyone."

Carla sat quietly, hoping that Michael had marked her essay. Thanks to Patricia she had finished it on Sunday evening ready to give to Michael first thing on Monday morning. She had hoped to give it to him herself but he was away at a conference, so she reluctantly left it with Mrs Madden, the faculty secretary. For the rest of the week she waited. As the room emptied Carla pretended to check her phone messages.

"Well done, Ms Bianco!"

Michael held out the clear plastic envelope. "An excellent first essay."

There was a large red sixty six percent on the front page.

Carla took it. "Thanks." Her eyes lit up, energised by Michael's praise.

"Have a good Christmas."

"Thank you. You too." Carla watched Michael slip out of the lecture hall. She was already looking forward to the next semester.

In a corner of the room Jenny chatted to a group of students. She looked tentatively at Carla, who beamed at her. Jenny ran over to Carla and gave her a hug.

*****

Boxing Day, and Carla had her usual houseful of family, friends and neighbours. The last ten days had disappeared in a flurry of Christmas shopping, the usual round of festivities, and shifts at the deli, bustling with Christmas shoppers taking the weight off their feet and their wallets. Gianni had closed at 2pm on Christmas Eve and decided to keep the deli closed until the New Year. The family needed some time off. He had arrived at Carla's with three large trays of lasagne, and a pile of containers filled with olives, cheeses, and salads. Mamma, Nina and Gina had made two of their huge vermouth soaked sponges. Bing Crosby crooned *White Christmas*, and her guest's faces glowed from alcohol, and the heat from the hearth.

Carla felt relaxed and happy as she meandered around the room topping up glasses. She was looking forward to spending time with her family, and planned to persuade Richard to take a few days off so the four of them could go to Centre Parks.

Jenny held a large empty glass. Her eyes were glazed.

"Martin loved Christmas," she sniffed.

Mamma Bianco, Nina and Gina nodded. Mamma picked up a bottle of red wine and filled Jenny's glass. She looked at her empty water glass and lifted the bottle. Angela swiped the bottle from Mamma Bianco.

"Not until your medication is sorted." Angela walked off taking the bottle with her.

Mamma poked her tongue out at Angela's back.

"*White Christmas*, was his favourite song." Jenny closed her eyes and sang along wildly off key.

Mamma gently lifted the glass out of Jenny's hand, took a swig and dropped it back into back into place.

At the other end of the room Carla topped up Nellie's wine. "How's Goldsmith's Nellie?"

"Bit of a culture shock at first. So different to Bath. The high street is full of these amazing stalls. There's always music coming from somewhere. I love it, it's brilliant."

"Oxford is just like Bath," moaned Isabella. "No it's worse."

"What do you mean?" Carla hadn't spoken to Isabella about Oxford since she got back. The Christmas rush at the deli had taken up every spare moment.

"My grades are crap and the course is sooo boring, just like the people on it," she moaned. "I'm supposed to be having the time of my life. Not."

"You will Bella. Give it a chance." Carla spotted some glasses that needed filling. She started to move towards them. "Come summer, I bet you won't want to come home."

Carla filled Brian's glass.

Brian raised his glass to Carla. "Here's to getting away from whingeing clients for a few days."

"As long as they keep bringing in the money they can whinge as much as they like." Richard raised his glass to his clients.

"Well, I'm looking forward to spending time with the twins," said Brian.

"That reminds me, why don't we all go to off for a few days with the kids ..." Carla was interrupted by a low burring sound.

Richard pulled out his mobile and checked the screen. "Excuse me." He walked towards the hall.

"I thought Centre Parks might be nice," continued Carla to herself.

Dean Martin was no match for Mamma Bianco, Nina and Gina. They swayed as they sang along to *That's Amore*. Jenny joined in with a slurred "la."

"They should audition for Britain's Got Talent," joked Brian, but Carla wasn't listening.

Her eyes were fixed on the figure in the hall. How rude of Richard to take a call when they had guests. Richard put his head round the door and beckoned to Carla. She walked over to him. This had better be important.

"Just got a call from Adam Peters. You remember, from the rugby. He's asked me to make up the numbers on a golf trip. Someone's dropped out." He looked like a child waiting to see if his mother would buy him a toy he really wanted.

"Is that all? When is it?"

"I leave tonight." Richard searched Carla's face trying to anticipate a reaction.

"What?"

Richard put his hand on Carla's shoulder. "I know it's short notice, but he's started putting a lot of business my way. I can hardly say no. It's not as if we've got anything planned." Richard was practised at sounding like the voice of reason.

"But Christmas isn't even over and I was hoping …"

"Carla, the more fees I bring into the company, the better chance I have of becoming senior partner. That's always been the plan. Besides, it'll give you more time to do some studying."

"That's very generous of you."

"It's important." Richard stroked Carla's cheek. "It's only a couple of days."

"You'd better go then."

"I'll go pack." Richard pecked Carla on the cheek and sauntered up the stairs.

Carla raised the champagne bottle she was still clutching and took a swig.

"You do that," she muttered to herself.

From the living room she heard a burst of voices. "That's amore."

Carla straightened up, put on a smile and re-joined the party.

*****

Chapter Four

Carla and Jenny sat transfixed. The final moments of Ibsen's *A Doll's House* was playing out on the stage of The Rondo Theatre where Michael had arranged a block booking for his students.

Nora declared to her husband that she needed to stand on her own two feet in order to find herself.

A lump formed in Carla's throat. She had already read the play, but *seeing* Nora in Victorian dress, about to leave her family, she saw what a shocking impact it would have had on the audience back in 1879. More than a hundred years on, Carla knew it wasn't a decision she would ever take. Unlike Nora she couldn't complain about having a controlling husband. Hers was more the absent husband. Richard had been true to his word about giving Carla time to study. During the past three months he would arrive home, grab a late supper and go straight to bed. That was when he hadn't already entertained clients at one of the new restaurants that opened at regular intervals in the city. Otherwise, life was good. Robbie had settled well into secondary school, Isabella had gone back to Oxford buoyed up by plans for her and Nellie to visit each other at weekends, and Mamma Bianco was being treated for high blood pressure and angina, and managed to do a few hours each day in the deli. The evenings were getting lighter, daffodils along grass verges had turned the world a cheerful yellow, and Carla had kept up with her with studies. Michael's Realism classes had started with Ibsen's *A Doll's House* and what he called the woman question, and had finished with Mamet's *Glengarry Glen Ross*, about a group of backstabbing estate agents. Some of the scenes in the plays had a familiarity that left Carla wondering whether in the hundred years between Ibsen and Mamet, men and women had evolved at all.

On stage, Nora picked up her bag and looked her husband in the eye.

Carla's eyes welled up.

Helmut took a step towards Nora, but she walked towards the door.

Helmut sank into a chair and put his head in his hands. He sobbed.

A door slammed. The curtain came down and the audience burst into applause. Jenny cheered.

Carla wiped the tears rolling down her cheeks with her hand. She wanted Nora to come back but she knew she wasn't going to. A hand appeared over her shoulder holding out a large tissue. Carla looked over her shoulder.

"Thanks." Carla took the tissue from Michael and blew hard.

The cast took their final bow.

Jenny got up. "I need a drink."

Jenny handed Carla a glass of white wine and gulped her vodka and coke.

"He could have arranged for us to see a comedy," said Jenny. "I feel like slitting my wrists," she added.

"Sorry," came a voice from behind her. "Comedy is on next year's syllabus. Until then it's grim realism."

Michael stood next to Jenny. Jenny raised her eyes to the ceiling. "Kill me now." She took another large gulp from her glass.

A man in his forties, with large brown eyes and a warm coffee coloured complexion appeared next Michael.

"This is Nathan McDonald, the theatre director."

Nathan's shy smile revealed perfect tombstone teeth.

"Hi."

"Fabulous production." Jenny drained the glass.

"Really great," confirmed Carla.

"They're all local amateurs. This is a community theatre and we're always looking for people to get involved."

"Ooh, count me in," Jenny chirped.

Carla cocked her head towards Jenny at this unexpected offer.

"It'll make a change from staying in with a bottle of wine," Jenny added.

"Great. Come along next Tuesday, seven thirty." Nathan looked at Carla.

"I'd love to but ..."

"You've got better things to do?"

"Family commitments," explained Carla. Her life was finally under control and she didn't want to risk biting off more than she could chew.

Jenny looked into her empty glass.

"Would you like another drink," offered Michael.

"Yes, please."

Carla looked at her watch. "Sorry Jen, got to go. I have to be at the deli at the crack of dawn tomorrow."

"You're the chauffer." Jenny plonked her empty glass in Nathan's hand. "See you Tuesday."

"Great."

Michael held out his hand to relieve Carla of her glass.

"Parker?" Jenny chuckled.

"Ready when you are Miss Penelope."

Carla and Jenny dissolved into the throng surrounding the bar. Michael felt a tinge of disappointment. He looked down at the wine glass in his hand. Around the rim was berry red print of Carla's bottom lip.

Nathan looked and Michael raising his eyebrows.

"What?" asked Michael. "My interest is purely professional."

"I didn't say a word," teased Nathan.

"She's married. It would be professionally inappropriate, and you know I'm crap at relationships."

"It wasn't your fault your first wife ran off with a lesbian," said Nathan patting Michael on the back with mock reassurance. "On the other hand …"

A couple of bemused faces turned towards the men.

"Thanks mate." Michael lifted Carla's glass to his mouth and emptied it. He tasted the rose scented lipstick on his lips and wondered what it would be like to taste the real thing.

*****

It had been a hectic day at Bianco's Mangia Bene. Thanks to the influence of upmarket Italian chains like Carluccio's, the cupola shaped packages of panettone and the foot long bars of torrone were popular Easter gifts. The gentle spring sunshine had also attracted the groups of Bath ladies who lunch. With Richard out on a business dinner, and Robbie at a birthday sleepover, Carla looked forward a lavender bubble bath, a glass of Chianti and settling down to her umpteenth viewing of When Harry Met Sally. Gianni handed Carla a box filled with enough food to feed the entire cul de sac.

"Bye Gianni, see you next week." Carla closed the door behind her and squinted in the gentle evening sunshine.

"Hey Mum." Isabella leaned against the black railings along the riverside, a small backpack at her feet.

"Bella! What are you doing back? You don't finish for another week."

"Nice to see you too." Isabella picked up her backpack.

Carla put her arm around her daughter. "Of course, it's lovely to see you. Just unexpected."

They walked along the path towards the car park. Isabella looked pale and thin, *in need of some Bianco home cooking* thought Carla. She decided against pressing her daughter for an explanation until she'd had a good feed.

As the front door closed behind them Isabella dropped her bag in the hall. She then relieved her mother of the food parcel, and loaded a plate with meatballs, mushroom risotto, and baked aubergines. Carla had nicknamed her the hoover. Thank goodness for Gianni. There was plenty to keep her fed and happy until Carla packed her back off to Oxford.

"I needed a break," explained Isabella, wedging a whole meatball into her mouth.

"Tell me about it. I've been on my feet since seven this morning."

"To tell the truth, I'm having a few problems."

Carla poured milk into the two large mugs turning the tea a rich tan. She needed it strong. The evening sun began to disappear behind the trees that lined the small field behind the garden. Carla closed the French doors.

"Why didn't you say anything earlier?" Carla sighed. *Another problem to solve. Another person to keep afloat.* She felt nearer sixty than forty.

"I did," replied Isabella resentfully. "You weren't listening. I've already told you, I don't like Oxford. I don't want to go back."

"But it's only a few more weeks before the summer holiday. Surely you can keep going till then," urged Carla.

"I can't," Isabella protested. "I've got this huge Irish drama essay to do and I don't know where to start."

Carla's eyes softened. "Well I do," she said decisively.

Thankfully this was one problem she could solve. Michael Nolan had given a series of lunchtime lectures on Irish Drama, his favourite subject. His enthusiasm was infectious, and she'd attended every one. She'd also taken pages of notes to help with future assignments.

"And when we've finished," continued Carla, "I've the perfect treat."

Carla's notes were scattered around the dining room table.

"Now, make sure you include the sacredness of the family in the Catholic ethos of Friel's characters," Carla pointed halfway down a page.

Isabella wrote. It was early afternoon the following day, and Isabella already had a four-page essay plan on issues of identity and culture in the plays of Brian Friel.

"There. Done," said Carla brightly, praying Isabella wouldn't find another spanner to put in the works.

Isabella's shoulders relaxed with a sigh of relief. "Thanks mum, that's a load off my mind."

It was a load off Carla's too. Now for the next part of her plan. "Time for some fun."

Isabella laughed for the first time since she'd got home. "Are you bribing me?"

"Shamelessly."

Carla handed Isabella her backpack. The station platform was quiet. The commuters had departed a couple of hours earlier. Carla's bribe: a back massage and a couple of new summer dresses, one cornflower blue, the other a sunny yellow, had sealed the deal.

"Thanks mum. I'll get the essay in on time now." A healthy blush had returned to Isabella's cheeks.

The train doors slammed shut.

"You're not allowed home until you do," teased Carla. She meant it. "It's only a few more weeks Bella. Get your exams out of the way and everything will be fine. I promise you."

Carla waved her daughter off. She skipped down the stairs back towards the station entrance and clapped her hands. Potential disaster averted. It would have been bad enough dealing with Isabella dropping out of university, but Richard's reaction would have made it even worse. The last thing Carla needed right now were any more distractions. All she wanted to do was get her head down and get on with her own studies.

*****

Carla raised her cheek to Richard's face. "Wish me luck."

Richard looked blank. He was halfway out the front door, and already running late for his first client.

"First year results. They're out today." Carla's stomach was doing somersaults and her bladder was on overdrive.

Easter had come and gone. Under the warm sun, the daffodils in the front garden had been replaced by blood red peonies. Carla could only look on with envy as the young women on campus abandoned their thick tights, exposing every inch of leg in their micro skirts. She reassured herself that she was still slim, but there was no getting away from it, these women were half her age. Neat black pedal pushers for her then, just on the knee. Her thighs were not for public consumption. Not that she'd had time to fret about it. She had been too busy meeting the essay deadlines before start of exams. Library books had been grabbed before the copies disappeared from the shelves, pages of notes taken, followed by the brain grinding task of attempting to organise the information into what the lecturers wanted; *a well researched, articulate and eloquent piece of work, well thought out critical analysis and original responses.* Thankfully Isabella seemed to have settled back down in Oxford, Robbie made the most of the dry weather by kicking a ball around the nearby field with the twins after school, and Richard was working harder than ever. Carla had met all her deadlines and survived her first year at university. How well she had survived, would be revealed in half and hour.

"You'll be fine." Richard pecked Carla mechanically on the cheek. "Tell you what ..." He put his hand inside his jacket and took out his wallet. With a small flourish he handed Carla two fifty-pound notes. "Celebrate. Have lunch, go shopping."

Carla melted. She put her arms around Richard's neck and kissed him on the lips. "I'm thinking something smooth and silky," she cooed.

Richard smiled, pleased with himself. "I'll try and get home early." He peeled Carla's arms from around his neck. "I'm running late."

Carla watched Richard's BMW turn right out of the cul de sac. He'd given her all the space she needed to do her own thing over the last few months, and had been understanding when she wanted to duck out of corporate functions. She promised herself she would make it up to him over the summer break, starting next weekend, by throwing a barbecue for everyone in his department.

"Sorry to spoil your afternoon," Patricia groaned holding her head in her hands. "My skull is splitting."

Carla pulled into her drive. Her car was full of bags. Some were tiny, the contents bought with Richard in mind, others were much larger, containing the latest additions to Carla's summer wardrobe. Her favourite buy was a purple empire line dress. Richard's cash had covered the bill at The Royal Crescent Hotel. It was Carla's way of thanking Patricia for taking Robbie off her hands too many times to count. The credit card melt down in New Southgate was to celebrate a great end to her first year. The hard work had paid off.

Carla turned off the engine and put her hand on Patricia's arm. "You haven't spoiled a thing. I've passed my exams, and shopped till I've dropped and ..."

Carla saw Richard's car was in the drive. He said he would get home early, but this was really impressive.

"And my darling husband has come home early. That's a pretty perfect day. Now let me get you some paracetamol."

As Carla turned the key in her front door she imagined Richard standing the other side of it smiling proudly, ready to take her in his arms. As soon as she had picked up her results Carla had sent him a text: *Off to celebrate!* Richard had texted her back: *Well done baby, have fun.*

And all the time he had planned to be there when she got home.

"Honey, I'm home," sang Carla doing her best Shania Twain impression, clashing with the big ballad booming from the living room.

"He's not going to hear you with that racket." Patricia walked towards the living room, desperate to turn it off. "And since when did Richard become a Westlife fan?"

Carla skipped up the stairs to her bedroom with her bulging carrier bags. She decided to hide a couple of them away for a few weeks, and bring the outfits out gradually, getting Richard to admire them, just before the credit card bill came through. Richard's dark blue suit jacket hung over the banister at the top of the stairs. It was a hot sticky afternoon. He was probably cooling off in the shower. She'd slip the bags into her wardrobe behind her winter coats, then, surprise him.

Carla quietly opened the bedroom door and stepped in. She stood motionless at the scene on her bed.

"Y-e-s, just there. Keep going."

Carla recognised the voice under Richard. Richard continued thrusting and grunting.

"I'm ... " he arched his back. His reflection rose into the large art deco mirror above the curved chrome headrest. He got a kick out of watching himself orgasm. He looked into the mirror, his eyes rolling back into his head. Westlife was suddenly silent. He paused for a second and caught sight of something in the mirror. He looked over his shoulder.

"Fuucck!" he yelled in a mixture of agony and ecstasy. He rolled to one side and looked over at the door. His flushed face turned deathly pale.

"Jesus!" Camilla pulled the chiffon blindfold from her eyes. "Have you slipped a disc?" She tossed the lavender scarf over the side of the bed and it floated slowly to the floor.

Carla recognised it. A present from Richard's golf trip at Christmas. The golf trip for which he had nearly forgotten to pack his clubs. She felt calm, as if she'd stepped out of her body, and was watching a scene from a film.

Camilla propped herself up on her elbows. Her eyes locked with Carla's. A split second look of surprise, then the corners of her mouth curled upwards. She stared at Carla. A look of devilish pleasure.

Carla's legs began to shake. Her heart pounded. It was difficult to breath.

"I think it's time for Chlamydia to leave," she said calmly, looking impassively at a terrified Richard. Carla was determined not to betray any emotion. "You look like you've had your money's worth."

Camilla coolly slid out of Carla's bed, picked up her dress and flounced, triumphant, past Carla.

Richard waited for Carla to react. He wouldn't know which way to play it until she did. Carla was paralysed. She looked down on herself, at a crossroads. Whatever she did now would shape the rest of her life.

"You shit!" Patricia screamed, running into the bedroom.

Richard shielded himself with his arms as Patricia hit him around the head with a rolled up Big Issue.

"Christ!" he yelped. "Get off me."

Patricia continued delivering the blows. "Just thank your lucky stars, I'm not carrying a couple of bricks you lying toe rag. Your *wife* doesn't deserve this, arsehole."

"Isn't she supposed to be doing that?" Richard protested.

Patricia stopped. Silence. Patricia and Richard looked at Carla for a reaction. Carla took a deep breath.

"Your *wife* is the one who tells you to pack your bags and leave." Carla ran from the room. A tsunami of emotion flooded her body. Tears rolled down her cheeks.

"Carla!" Patricia chased after her.

Carla was in the middle of her front lawn. She had come to a standstill, not knowing what to do next. Carla collapsed into the arms that wrapped themselves around her. Her body shook with deep sobs. Patricia stroked her hair.

"I'm so sorry Carla," Patricia whispered.

She led Carla across the drive to her front door.

"I'll let you know when the coast is clear." Patricia led Carla into the house. "God, I need paracetamol, my head is fucking killing me."

*****

Carla dapped her red eyes with a soggy tissue. The sunlight stung her salty cheeks. Most of the students had gone for the summer. The campus was a ghost town. Jenny sat opposite Carla on one of the picnic benches outside the Student's Union. The previous morning a large group of drama students had been clustered around the same table, talking excitedly about their plans for the summer. Jenny had felt envious of them, and also Carla, who had her family to fill the void over the summer. Twenty-four hours later, her friend's world had fallen to pieces. Nearly two years ago her own life had ground to a halt in the short seconds Martin's consultant uttered the words *inoperable brain tumour*. She squeezed Carla's hand.

"He promised he'd never cheat on me again, the lying shit." Carla tore at her tissue. "It's not something you ever really get over. You learn to live with it. Put on a smile. Remind yourself you're not allowed to beat him up over it. Put up and shut up."

Jenny nodded.

"So why do I feel guilty? He'll do it again Jen, if I let him. How many times before enough is enough?"

Jenny handed Carla a fresh tissue. "That's your call, Carla."

Carla got up. "I'm sorry, I need to be on my own for a bit."

"Don't be. I'm here if you need me."

"Thanks."

Carla walked slowly towards the lake. She felt exhausted, and needed somewhere green and quiet to think. Richard had left the house within the hour. When she checked the wardrobes she saw he had taken enough to see him through several affairs. She decided not to say anything to Robbie and Isabella for the moment. It was easy to make up excuses for Richard's absence. She had been doing it for the last ten years, ever since he'd become a partner at FalconQueen.

The trees around the lake created a gentle shade. Carla sat on the dark wooden bench that overlooked the still glassy waters. The distant bleating of sheep and the overhead chirruping high up in the trees soothed her. She closed her eyes and breathed deeply.

At the other end of the lake Michael and Nathan sat under a tree.

"Starting a writer's group is a great idea," Michael told Nathan.

"How do you fancy getting involved with putting the new plays on stage?" asked Nathan.

"Are you trying to get me acting again? You know I-"

"I know you gave up when your wife left. Michael, that was-"

"Give me two minutes." Michael had caught sight of a solitary figure on the bench near the lakeside.

Nathan looked in the direction of Michael's gaze.

"Would that be two professional minutes?" he smiled.

Michael walked briskly towards Carla. The crunching on the gravel path made Carla look up.

"I just wanted to say, well done." Michael had jogged the last few metres and was panting lightly.

Carla's face creased and she burst into tears. Not the reaction Michael was expecting. He sat down beside her.

"I'm guessing those are not tears of joy."

Carla sobbed harder. Michael put his arm around her shoulder. On the other side of the lake, Nathan thought Michael was finally making a move on Carla, and gave him a thumbs up. Michael ignored him.

"Whatever it is Carla, I'm sure it can be sorted."

"I'm married to a two timing shit. Sort that," Carla wailed. She clung tightly onto Michael.

Nathan had stood up. He was doing a hip grinding celebratory dance. Michael waved him off to stop, to no effect. He was still trying to take in Carla's bombshell, and didn't know what to say.

"I'm sorry," he managed.

Carla looked up at him. He could feel her breath on his neck. A hot air balloon almost directly above them let out a low rumble.

"I'd give anything to be up there." Carla raised her eyes. "Fly away."

Carla's mouth was inches away from Michael's. Talk about bad timing. Michael glanced over at Nathan who now had his arms across his body, stroking his sides and puckering his lips. Michael glared at him. Carla became calmer. She pulled herself away, embarrassed. She looked over in Nathan's direction. Nathan jumped out of his pose and pretended to examine the leaves on a nearby branch.

"Nathan's waiting for you. I should let you go."

"Listen, if you need time to work things out, you can always put your studies on hold," suggested Michael.

"Some things are past working out." Carla had to admit it. Richard had damaged their marriage past the point of no return. "Being here, getting on with my degree is the only thing that makes any sense."

"Okay." Michael got up. "You've got a few months to make up your mind. You can let me know at the end of the summer." Having been through a divorce himself Michael knew Carla would be in for a rough time.

"Thank you. I'm fine. Really."

"Look after yourself, Carla." Michael walked towards Nathan, who'd given up chivvying Michael into kissing Carla, and lay on his back trying to pick out faces in the puffy white clouds passing over the tops of the trees.

The hot air balloon let out another low hiss. Carla looked up and bit her lip.

*****

The July sun was trapped behind dense grey cloud. Carla and Patricia walked briskly along the riverside path. Opposite them, in Parade Gardens, a handful of sturdy pensioners sat in deckchairs and drank tea from flasks. The Courts were a five minute walk away. Five minutes away from rewriting the future Carla had always imagined for herself; the one where she and Richard lived happily ever after into cosy old age.

Robbie had taken the news of the split badly. Curled up on Richard's lap he had cried, hard. Carla looked on in silence, angry, unspeakably angry. Over the following weeks however, Richard had made efforts to spend time with Robbie, taking him go karting and golfing. Richard's new challenge was to be the perfect divorced Dad. Every outing was an opportunity to show the world what a great guy he was. For Robbie's sake Carla hoped Richard would keep it up.

Isabella wasn't as pliable as her younger brother. After her exams she'd gone to spend a couple of weeks with Nellie in New Cross. Carla wanted to wait until Isabella got home before breaking the news. Patricia had gone to the railway station around lunchtime to pick the girls up. They were stopped at a set of traffic lights when Nellie said, "Bella is that your Dad? ... oh, shit!"

Isabella looked out to the window. Richard was sat outside a café. He had his arm around Camilla and was

71

nibbling her ear. The lights turned green Patricia screeched away. By the time Isabella walked in through the front door she was beside herself.

"Why didn't you tell me? I hate him. What is he doing with that- that thing?"

Carla told Isabella the truth. It was one thing to shield Robbie. Isabella was an adult. And, Carla was sick of people looking at her as though there was something wrong with *her*.

Isabella was adamant. "I don't want anything to do with him."

The clouds spat out a fine drizzle.

"Are you sure about this?" ventured Patricia. Richard may have been a shit but she didn't want Carla to rush into something she might regret.

"Yes."

"You're still wearing your wedding ring," observed Patricia.

Carla held out her left hand and looked at the gold band. She felt nothing. Her heart had turned to stone. In a second the ring was off her finger. She tossed it high. Moments later it disappeared into the brown river Avon.

"No, I'm not," Carla answered tartly. "It was his mother's. I thought he was being sentimental. Cheapskate."

The women walked in silence to the busy main road and through the pillared entrance to the Courts. At the dark wooden doors Carla stopped. She looked at Patricia, suddenly scared. Patricia took her arm.

"Don't worry." Patricia led Carla through the door.

"I-I don't want to lose the house," Carla stammered. "They'll let me keep the house won't they?"

"Of course they will. It's in the best interest of you and the children. And Richard's not living there. You'll be fine," Patricia reassured her. "The courts are there to protect you and the children, you'll see."

Patricia was right, Carla told herself. She'd done nothing wrong. Life would carry on as it always had, just without Richard. Carla put a determined smile on her face, straightened up, and walked resolutely down the corridor to meet her solicitor.

Three hours later Carla and Patricia stepped out into the blinding sunshine. The grey clouds had broken up revealing an intensely blue sky, which failed to brighten Carla's deathly pallor.

"That judge has got his hand up someone's skirt, and it's not his wife's." The words caught in Carla's throat as she fought back the tears.

"I'm so sorry." Patricia put her arm around Carla's shoulders. "Sodding Judge, sodding solicitor, sodding boys network with their sodding rounds of golf and dodgy handshakes. Makes me want to vomit."

The court door opened. Richard and Camilla walked out arm in arm. Camilla tossed her peroxide hair. She was trying to grow it long. She had read in some magazine that mistresses always had longer hair than the wife, and she envied Carla's long glossy mane. As Richard and Camilla overtook Carla and Patricia, Camilla kissed Richard's cheek and gave Carla a triumphant smile. Richard coughed awkwardly and avoided eye contact.

"That soggy arse is definitely heading south," spat Patricia, glaring at Camilla as they crossed the road and headed into the car park.

The For Sale sign went up on Carla's lawn the next day. Carla felt the neighbour's pitying looks from behind their pruned hedges, not that she had time to think about the neighbours. As well as deciding she would sell her home, the judge, presumably as an incentive to do it quickly, had decided that Richard not longer responsible for paying the mortgage. Overnight she'd been made to feel like a second-

73

class citizen, the course of her life dictated by strangers who decreed that she was no longer worthy.

*****

A removal lorry loomed over Carla's drive. The *For Sale* sign had a *Sold* banner across it. The over grown front lawn was scattered with papery brown leaves. A short thickset man passed Carla's pine chairs to a thin young man in the back of the lorry. They slammed the back door shut and got in the cab. Carla watched them drive away.

Patricia came out of Carla's front door.

"I'll go ahead and let them in. Come along when you're ready," said Patricia.

"I'll have one last check." Carla stood in her doorway as Patricia got into her car.

"No rush." Patricia knew how hard it was for Carla to leave. She had always called number seven her dream home. When Richard had entertained fantasies about moving further out of Bath and playing lord of the manor, Carla had made it clear she had no intention of living, isolated, in some ivory tower in the middle of nowhere. She had grown up in the centre of town, and the neat lawns of her suburban cul de sac were countryside enough.

Carla watched Patricia follow the removal van. She closed the front door. The empty rooms filled with the sounds of memories. "Yeess" yelled Robbie as he scored on his computer game. Isabella's bedroom walls shook to the sound of her current favourite song. "You look lovely," whispered Richard standing at the bottom of the stairs in his dinner suit looking up at Carla. A gust of cold air blew in from the kitchen window and sucked the memories away. It was just a house, four walls and a roof. Carla closed the window, left the spare keys on the window ledge in the hall, and shut the front door behind her.

Patricia straightened a cushion and looked around the overcrowded living room. Thankfully, the day before, Isabella and Nellie had blanked out the eighties floral wallpaper with a couple of coats of magnolia.

"I'll have to get rid of some of this furniture," sighed Carla, squeezing through the narrow gap between two armchairs.

"It's cosy." Patricia tried to sound enthusiastic. She knew Carla preferred spacious to cosy.

"It's like going back twenty years with none of the benefits." Carla plonked herself in the armchair, exhausted. It had been a long miserable summer.

"Richard gets his credit card out, buys himself a new life, and I'm left clearing up the mess from the old one."

Patricia put her hand on Carla's shoulder. "You need some time to yourself," she said softly "I'll drop Robbie back later."

"Thanks."

The front door closed. Carla opened a cardboard box and took out a handful of books. She started to place them on the top shelf of the empty bookcase in the alcove next to the fireplace. Alcoves were something new. Richard had always preferred new houses with pristine featureless walls. New houses came at a premium, especially on the southern downs overlooking the green slopes of the Monkton Combe Valley. Carla's Edwardian terrace was less than 2 miles from her old house. It was important to her that Robbie stayed in familiar surroundings with of his friends living close by. When they had viewed the house Robbie was impressed that the second bedroom was big enough not only for the double bed he had inherited from the guest room of their old house, but also for the track of his model Flying Scotsman. The fact that he would finally have a bigger bedroom than his elder sister had sealed the deal.

Carla picked out a handful of books and placed them next to the ones on the shelf. In her hand was a colourful guide to Venice. A lilac envelope stuck out from behind the front cover. Carla opened the book. She pulled a handmade card from the envelope. Carla hadn't looked at it since she'd slipped it into the book ten years earlier. To find the strength to move forward with her life, some memories had to be buried, even if those memories carried a warning for the future. She opened the card. Inside, in his spidery handwriting Richard had written a big lie.

My Darling Carla
Thank you for giving us another chance.
You won't regret it.
All my love,
Richard xxx

The nineteen year old secretary with aspirations to marry a solicitor had been given an excellent reference and passed on to a firm in Bristol. There, she would continue to hone her predatory skills to dismantle the life of another frazzled mother, whose husband wined, dined and screwed her in an anonymous hotel several miles away.

Richard had given all the usual excuses. She had made a move on him, he was flattered, Carla was busy with the children. The fierce instinct to protect her family, to keep it intact in the face of Richard's infidelity, came as a shock to her. She had stopped the situation from spiralling out of control by keeping it from her family, confiding only in Patricia. In a few short weeks life had returned to normal. By that time Carla had brought her wardrobe up to date, got the convertible she'd always wanted, and joined the nearby country club. If an overgrown schoolgirl was going to make a play for her lifestyle, Carla was damn well going to make sure that she had a life worth aspiring to.

Relieved that he had got off lightly, Richard took Carla's spending spree on the chin and did his part by arranging a surprise trip to Venice. They had an overblown romantic four days, dinner beside the Grand Canal, a gondola ride through picturesque side streets lined with tiny shops crammed with lace jewellery and delicious pastries. And there was sex, lots of it. Richard was determined to put things right, and that included making sure Carla didn't feel the need to get her own back, secretly or otherwise. Revenge was the last thing on Carla's mind. All she wanted was to feel safe. Eventually she did. *What a fool.*

The shredded pieces of Richard's promises fell onto the carpet. There was no such thing as safe. Life was unsafe. She began to take her university books off the shelf. Michael was right. There was no point in trying to cope with university. The start of her second year was only a week away. It was going to take her more than a week to sort out the scrambled mess in her head. Carla dropped onto the sofa, curled up, and closed her eyes. She drifted into a dream. Isabella and Robbie were in the house with her. The house was listing at a forty-five degree angle and it was filling with water.

BRIIING! The piercing ring of the doorbell cut through Carla's body. Carla woke up with a jolt. That bell would have to go. The previous occupant may have been deaf but she wasn't. If it was a Jehovah's Witness hoping to convert her then, "I am a Catholic. Can I interest you in converting to Catholicism?" usually had them scurrying in the opposite direction. Carla opened the door.

Mamma Bianco was flanked by Gianni and Angela, who were both loaded down with boxes. Mamma kissed Carla on the cheek.

"Figlia mia, you need to eat." Mamma always uttered these words in times of crisis.

She burst past Carla and bustled through the hallway, instinctively making her way to Carla's kitchen.

"Hey sis." Gianni and Angela dutifully followed their mother into the kitchen.

Carla filled the heavy metal base of the espresso cafetiere with cold water. She'd make sure she used decaffeinated. Mamma Bianco was already in warp speed, pulling out slender bottles of extra virgin olive oil from a bag. Packets of pasta bows, quills and shells were already piled up on the counter.

"Disagraziato!" hissed Mamma slamming a thick short salami on wooden chopping board next to the sink, leaving her daughter in no doubt as to what she would do to Richard if she ever got her hands on him. "I never like him,"

Slam! The siblings jumped and looked in bemusement at the salami that lay in two perfect halves on the chopping board. Mamma waved the meat cleaver in her children's direction making her point.

"Ees smile, so false." The corners of Mamma's mouth widened showing her upper teeth in a grotesque imitation of Richard faking a smile.

"She's changed her tune," said Angela under her breath. "For twenty years the sun shone out of his arse."

In spite of herself, Carla laughed. Richard had Camilla, but that was all he had.

Having made her point with the salami Mamma Bianco set about chopping up a few cloves of garlic. Gianni located Carla's saucepans, grabbed the biggest and set to work alongside his mother.

Mamma Bianco nodded to Angela the way she did when some form of family business was afoot. "Angela, you tell Carla what we gonna do."

Angela smiled. Things were about to change. She wondered how Carla would react. "Mamma's decided we're going to run the deli without you."

"W-why? How?" spluttered Carla.

"I've always wanted to run a business, so I'm swapping accounting for the deli."

"You never said." Carla was bewildered.

"You never asked," laughed Angela. "Look, you gave up your education when Papa died, now it's our turn to support you. You've got enough on your plate without having to worry about the deli. And me and Gianni, we're ready for a change."

78

"That's right," agreed Gianni putting the finishing touches to a salad that wouldn't have looked out of place at the Tate Modern.

"What's Gianni changing?" asked Carla open mouthed.

"Michelangelo here has just started a part time art course," announced Angela feeling more like the oldest rather than the youngest sibling.

"Michelangelo," chuckled Mamma Bianco to herself, throwing a generous quantity of pasta quills into a pan of bubbling water.

"That's right," confirmed Gianni, "I went for an interview, showed them my portfolio and that was it. I'm going to hang my paintings in the deli- my own ready made art gallery."

"You have a portfolio?" Carla was beginning to wonder whether she'd been living in a parallel universe. Was anybody who she thought they were?

"I always said his brains were in his hands." Angela made to pluck a slice of cucumber from Gianni's work of art. Gianni slapped her hand.

"I don't know what to say," Carla looked at amazement at her family. "That's fantastic."

Mamma Bianco stirred the penne. Carla had been so wrapped up in herself over the last few months that she hadn't noticed her mother had aged, the way people did when they were anxious or worried.

"Is she okay?" Carla whispered to Angela.

"The high blood pressure is under control and she's taking drugs for the angina."

"With the divorce and the move, I'm not helping am I?" murmured Carla guiltily.

"What were you supposed to do Carla? Dick For Brains moved straight in with that bitch. Played right into her money grabbing claws. Mamma will be fine. You'll see."

Mamma took her wooden spoon to the pan full of thick red pasta sauce and continued stirring. Her face, warmed by the rising steam, began to lose its pallor.

Mamma started humming *Volare*, her voice clear and light. Gianni joined in with the *oh oh oh*'s in his best smudgy Dean Martin impression, as he grated a huge chunk of fresh parmesan. Angela laid out the tablemats, joining in. Taking Mamma Bianco in his arms, Gianni danced her around Carla's kitchen. The heaviness in Carla's heart began to lift. *Watch out Rat Pack the Bianco's are in town.* She joined in the final chorus. From his cage in the corner Lellow the canary finally broke his silence and chirped with gusto. The kitchen was filled the aroma of basil, parsley, garlic and the fresh coffee that gurgled up in the cafetiere. It smelt like home. Carla promised herself that after supper she would put all her university books back on the shelf. Angela was right she had given up her education once before. It was time to finish what she had started.

*****

The cheap wardrobe Gianni and Robbie had assembled in Carla's bedroom, listed slightly as she dragged a large suitcase off the top. The solid beech wardrobes she'd left behind were being enjoyed by their new owners she thought with a wry smile. But this was no time for looking back. Over the last week Carla, Isabella, and Robbie had put up blinds, mown the small lawns and given the front door a fresh coat of white paint.

The previous owner had lived on her own in the property for many years. During that time she had lost her sight, but as Carla transformed the house she felt the old lady's presence. The presence watched them with a sense of amusement. Carla knew that when she was ready the spirit would move on, but she kept this thought to herself. She didn't want her children to think their mother had completely lost it.

Carla popped her head around Isabella's bedroom door. Isabella pressed the blu tack on the back of a Salavador Dali poster against the wall over her bed. Gone was the double bed, the ensuite, and fitted furniture. Poor Bella, she hadn't had a room this small since she was a baby thought Carla. A twinge of guilt pinched her heart.

"I thought you'd like help packing." Carla put the suitcase on Isabella's bed.

Isabella pulled the blu tack away from the wall and adjusted the poster.

"It's alright, you don't need to."

"You hate packing."

"Then it's a good job I won't be." Poster in place Isabella faced Carla.

"What?" Carla didn't understand.

"Packing. It's a good job I won't be packing. I'm not going back," said Isabella matter of factly. It was the fait accompli tone she adopted when she had made a decision she knew was going to encounter opposition.

"What do you mean you're not going back? You've rented a flat. It's all sorted." Carla's mouth went dry and her heart beat faster, the way it always did lately when life felt out of control.

Isabella continued in a nonchalant tone. "One of the other students took my place."

Carla felt wobbly. She sank onto Isabella's bed. Her resistance to upset had become almost non-existent over the last few months. All reserves of strength had long been drained.

"Bella, you have to finish your degree," she pleaded.

"No I don't," snapped Isabella. "I hate Oxford. I wish I'd gone to Goldsmith's with Nellie. I just scraped through my exams, and if I didn't fit in before, now it's going to be ten times worse."

"What do you mean?"

"Mum, they all live in huge houses and/"

"Like we used to," finished Carla. She felt like a bucket of cold water had been thrown over her.

Isabella looked down at the ugly patterned carpet.

"Forget it," Isabella muttered, "It's not important."

"Then why do I feel it is?" Carla looked into her daughter's unhappy face. She felt helpless. Mothers were supposed to make everything right.

Isabella sat on the bed next to Carla. "You've had enough to deal with," she said gently. "I want to stay here with you and Robbie. This is where I'm needed. I can help out at the deli till I sort myself out. Mum, how is that any different from what you did?"

Carla was silenced. She'd planted the seeds for this moment over twenty years ago. This was all her fault.

*****

Chapter Five

Michael stood at the front of the lecture hall introducing this semester's comedy module. He had spent most of the summer in Dublin. Apart from Nathan he didn't have any friends in Bath, and he had missed the intimacy of meeting someone he knew every time he walked down the street or went into his local. Over the summer break he had sometimes wondered whether he would see Carla sitting in the lecture hall when he got back. And there she was, hiding at the back, pale and drawn. She was obviously having a difficult time, and probably not in the best frame of mind for a lecture on comedy.

"So," continued Michael winding up his talk, "I hope you all had a good break because last year was a practice run, and now is when it really starts to count. If you have any problems along the way, come and see me, before it's too late."

Jenny gave Carla a worried glance. They had met in the refectory before the lecture, where Carla had told Jenny about Isabella's surprise announcement. Jenny could see it had really knocked the stuffing out of her. When they had met up over the summer Carla had always managed to make a dry joke about her situation. But Isabella's news had left her dazed and lost.

"See you in class," Michael concluded.

The hall filled with the excited babble of friends reuniting, making their way to the Union bar.

Jenny stood up. Carla remained slumped in her seat, her pen still hovering over her pad, with barely two sentences to show for the hour.

"How about a cup of tea?" coaxed Jenny "Go down well with those giant cup cakes they've started selling. My treat."

Carla forced a smile and looked up at her friend. She was surprised to see Michael standing behind Jenny. He looked straight at Carla.

"Can I have a word?" There was a hint of anxiety in his voice.

"I'll wait outside," said Jenny.

Jenny gave Michael a look that reflected his concern, and slipped away. Michael looked around to make sure they were out of earshot of any of stragglers. He sat down next to her. The last time he had spoken to Carla she may have been upset, but her spirit was strong. Now she looked completely dejected. She couldn't even meet his eyes.

"Carla, I don't mean to pry, but ..."

"I look like shit." Carla stared down at her hands, which were clenched together into a tight ball in her lap.

"How are you doing?"

Carla now looked directly at Michael. "I've had to sell my home and disrupt my children's lives, and I was doing just fine, until yesterday." The shock of Isabella's decision was beginning to wear off. Now she felt angry. "Which was when my daughter decided to drop a bombshell of her own."

Michael sat next to Carla and waited for her to continue. Carla realised that the person she was angry with was herself and it was unfair to take it out on Michael. She moderated her tone.

"She's dropped out of Oxford. She's been really miserable there." Carla explained. "Said she should have gone to Goldsmith's all along. It's my fault, I pushed her to stick out her first year."

"You did the right thing Carla," Michael reassured her. "Give me a couple of days, I'll see if I can come up with any ideas."

Michael stood up. Carla shook her head.

"It's no use. She's not going back."

*****

The Royal Crescent was bathed in autumn sun. Jenny and Carla walked past the elegant columned buildings that looked out onto a vast empty lawn. The celebratory lunch at The Royal Crescent Hotel with Patricia, when she passed her first year at university, felt like a memory from another life. They entered Victoria Park through an iron gateway. Jenny had suggested they take a walk and then pop into her house for a bite to eat. Carla looked like she could do with some fresh air to put some of colour back in her cheeks. She also wanted to find a way of getting Carla out of the house more, meet some new people and have some fun.

"Hey," said Jenny casually, "let's go into the Botanical Gardens, I'll show you where we did our outdoor production of *A Midsummer Night's Dream*."

Jenny strode ahead taking a sharp right on a small path, bordered with plants of all shapes and sizes.

"Sorry, I didn't get to see it," muttered Carla remembering her manners. She was on autopilot and couldn't care less she had missed the play.

Jenny strode in front. She stopped halfway along a path. A huge evergreen towered over the broad lawn in front of her.

"Right in front of the tree, that was our stage. The audience sat all around us picnicking, with their kids being chased by the fairies. It was great fun."

"Sounds it." Carla nodded trying to sound vaguely interested. All she could think about was that Isabella was at home in that pokey bedroom when she should have been unpacking her stuff in a flat in Oxford.

Jenny's face brightened as if she'd just had a great idea. "Listen, why don't you come to the play reading at the The Rondo tomorrow night? Help us decide what to do for our next production."

"Thanks, Jen but I'm not really in the mood for that kind of thing," replied Carla flatly.

"Oh, come on, it'll be fun."

"Just let me get to grips with getting back to studying, then I'll think about it, okay?"

"I just thought the break would do you good, that's all."

Something snapped. Carla faced Jenny. Dejection had turned to anger. Nobody seemed to have a clue how she felt. Since the divorce her life had become unrecognisable. She hadn't just lost her home, she'd lost her life. It had become clear to her that she'd become a social pariah. The phone rarely rang, invitations had mysteriously dried up, and women she'd once been on friendly terms with couldn't get away fast enough when she bumped into them in town, especially if they were with their husbands. All that, she could put up with, but not the thought that Isabella and Robbie were going to pay the price for her divorce.

"Oh, I need a break alright," Carla said sharply. "I have to watch every penny I spend, my son sobs himself to sleep, and my daughter is ruining her future. Every morning I wake up sick to my stomach wondering what the hell happened. So please, give me a break."

Carla's outburst caught Jenny by surprise. She'd forgotten how resistant she had been to the efforts of well meaning friends who had tried to bring her out of her depression after Martin's death, how she thought they just didn't understand what she was going through. Now she'd done the same to Carla. At least she had happy memories to remember Martin by.

"Sorry, I just wanted to help," Jenny said quietly.

Carla felt dreadful. She had attacked one of the few friends that hadn't fallen off the radar.

"Sorry, I didn't mean to snap," whispered Carla digging her heels into the gravel.

Jenny took Carla's arm and led her out of the park.

Two days later Carla sat in Michael's office. Her stomach was in knots as she listened to him explain Isabella's situation with someone called Peter. Michael seemed to know Peter pretty well judging from the ribbing he gave him about some book he'd just had published.

Isabella had kept out of Carla's way since her announcement, preferring to spend her days at the deli helping Angela and Gianni, and her evenings at a fitness studio doing street dancing, belly dancing and possibly pole dancing, for all Carla knew. Carla hoped she could get Isabella back into fulltime education before her daughter decided to embark on a career as a burlesque dancer.

"Thanks Peter. I'll email you later."

"What did he say?" Carla was bursting.

Michael's smile, creased the corners of his eyes. "There's a place for her at Goldsmiths. She can go straight into the second year."

Carla leapt off her chair. Her face lit up. The load she had been carrying on her shoulders lifted.

"I don't know what to say."

For a second she made to hug Michael but immediately put her arms by her sides. It probably wasn't a good idea to end up in the arms of her tutor every time she felt emotional. The hug at the lakeside was a one off. "Thank you," she beamed.

"It's my pleasure," replied Michael looking suddenly bashful.

Carla sauntered towards the door.

"By the way," Michael added.

Carla felt a wave of panic flood her body. "Yes?"

"You don't look like shit." He gave Carla a cheeky grin.

Carla laughed. Shame the hugging thing was a one off. She slipped out of the office and closed the door behind her.

"Well?" said Jenny hopping up and down, "What did he say?"

Carla's face glowed. A light bulb had switched on inside her. "He said I didn't look like shit."

Jenny screwed up her eyes, confused.

"What?"

"Come on." Carla hooked her arm into Jenny's and led her down the corridor. "The cup cakes are on me."

*****

Carla stepped out of the main entrance of Goldsmiths University. Grey clouds released a persistent spray that failed to dampen Carla's mood. Isabella hadn't needed any convincing to transfer to Goldsmiths. Nellie had come home for the weekend just to make sure Isabella didn't back track. She insisted that Isabella move in with her until she sorted herself out. Patricia played chauffeur. Carla had very little driving experience outside of Bath. Richard had always belittled Carla's driving skills and had insisted on driving when they were out together. Patricia knew Carla would be eaten alive by London drivers.

"What do you think?" asked Carla.

Isabella's twinkling eyes said it all.

"I love it, I really do." Isabella looked around taking it all in. "And it's all thanks to ... what's his name?"

"Michael," supplied Carla.

A look of concern crossed Isabella's face. Carla picked up on it in a nano second. The turmoil of the last few months had left her hypersensitive.

"But? Please don't tell me there's a but," she pleaded.

"What about you?" asked Isabella.

Relief quickly replaced the flood of anxiety. Patricia got in first.

"Your mother will be fine," she reassured Isabella firmly.

"Time to go Bella," chipped in Nellie. "We've got a class in two minutes." She winked at Carla.

Carla hugged Isabella and winked back over her daughter's shoulder. The girls waved goodbye as they entered the building.

"And just remember," said Patricia waving back, "everyone is a potential murderer."

Carla elbowed Patricia.

"Ouch!"

Isabella and Nellie burst out laughing and disappeared into the building.

"Better safe than sorry," reasoned Patricia.

*****

With Isabella settled at Goldsmiths Carla felt ready to face the academic year ahead. The structure gave her a sense of purpose. Apart from Patricia and her family, she saw no one from her old life. But with her days spent on campus, and evenings running Robbie around and writing essays, she hardly noticed. Gianni and Angela had Bianco's Mangia

Bene under control. Mamma was allowed to help with food preparation in the mornings but was sent off to hang out with Nina and Gina in the afternoons. They made the most of their free bus passes and explored the villages and hamlets around Bath. Mamma always made sure she had leaflets offering a ten percent discount on the deli menu to hand out to everyone they met. With a mischievous glint in her eye she told them she was head of business development.

Carla avoided contact with Richard. In her heart she knew he would always try to undermine her. It was important to keep looking forward and focus on the future. Before she knew it the veil of snow that had transformed the campus into a magical wonderland in January, had given way to the waxy magnolia petals that carpeted the lawns. They were blown away by the blustery April winds revealing clusters of daisies with pink tipped heads gazing up to the sharp June sun.

From a distance, Michael watched Carla grow stronger as she regained her confidence. She had made the right decision not to give up her studies. He knew from experience that getting through the first year of divorce was a milestone. She was through the worst.

A group of excited students crowded around a notice board. There was a lot of shrieking and hugging. Carla and Jenny managed to claw their way to the front. They had just enough time to run their fingers down the list and glimpse their marks before they were bumped out of the way by other anxious students.

"Yes!" Jenny cried out giving Carla a tight hug and jumping up and down at the same time.

Carla felt a huge sense of relief. "That's a pretty good birthday present, even if it is my fortieth."

Some of the students threw Carla a look of pity. Forty was old. They were a million years from being forty.

"You kept that quiet," said Jenny. "I mean- happy birthday!"

"Thanks."

"You must have something special planned." Jenny couldn't help feeling put out that she hadn't been invited. For months, she and Carla had seen each other nearly every day.

"We're having a big family lunch on Sunday at the deli. I'd like you to come. Sorry I didn't ask you earlier, I think I've been trying to block it out."

Jenny didn't need asking twice. She loved the madness of Carla's family gatherings. It was so different from the dry restrained atmosphere between her and her mother. "I'd love to, but it's your birthday today. You must do something today."

Carla shrugged. Before the divorce there would have been lots of phone calls from her friends with invitations to dinner. This year, no one called. Jenny read Carla's face. It wasn't difficult to work out what had, or rather hadn't happened. She'd been through the same thing herself.

"Right," she said taking control. "You're coming out with me tonight. I know just the place."

A berry red gloss put the finishing touch to Carla's makeup. She stood in front of the mirror for a final check. Her favourite black and white flower print skirt ended on the knee and showed off her smooth tanned legs. That afternoon she had treated herself to a full leg wax. The beautician had thrown in a half price Brazilian, not that Carla's love life required such attention to detail. She eyed herself critically. Something wasn't quite right with her camisole. The penny dropped.

"Barely forty and they're already sagging," she muttered to herself.

Reaching inside her top, she shortened both bra straps. Boobs in the right place, she gave them a gentle pat.

"Much better. Surgery can wait."

Grabbing her fringed bag, Carla skipped down the stairs. Robbie was staying over at the deli. He enjoyed hanging out with Gianni, who would spend hours sharing his newly acquired art techniques with his nephew. Isabella had rung earlier that evening. She was relieved to hear her mother had something arranged for her birthday. She desperately wanted to come home to be with Carla but couldn't get the time off from her waitressing job in a posh Greenwich restaurant.

Carla closed the front door and crossed the road to her car. What a difference a year made. It was around this time the previous year that Carla had pulled into her drive, and her whole life had turned on a moment. If someone had asked her on her thirtieth birthday how she thought she would be spending her fortieth, she would not have answered, *in a quiet country pub with a thirty seven year old widow* she had known for less than two years. But Carla was more than happy to have a quiet evening with her new best friend. Jenny may have been her newest friend but she was also one of the most loyal, and that was worth more to her than some pretentious party full of fakes.

The country pub Jenny had chosen was in the green valley just a couple miles from Carla's house. The small car park was nearly full. Carla parked in the middle of the last three empty spaces. She always seemed to need twice as much space as everyone one else to park. As for reversing, travelling backwards whilst steering and looking over her shoulder, that really messed with her brain.

Carla checked her phone. *In the taxi. Mine's a G and T. Jen xx.* Carla smiled to herself. She made her way down the steep steps to the entrance of The Hope and Anchor. The buzz of chatter and laughter greeted her the other side of the door. A long table with a party of about ten people caught her eye. A double take stopped her dead. She felt like she'd been caught in a vortex and sucked into the past. One by one the faces around the table looked up and stared in Carla's direction. Richard pretended to look uncomfortable, Camilla relished every second silently toasting Carla with a glass of red wine, Patricia looked mortified, whilst former neighbours and friends were red faced and open mouthed. Behind Carla, two men standing at the bar caught the scene. Michael put down his pint. He had spotted Carla the moment she came smiling through the door. Now she stood frozen, staring a group of people who were staring back at her. Michael didn't have a clue what was going on but something was very wrong, and Carla was outnumbered.

Carla scanned the table. Her eyes panned back. She looked in disbelief at Patricia. Patricia's mouth opened and closed.

"Carla, I-I" she finally stammered.

An arm circled Carla's shoulder.

"I was beginning the wonder where you'd got to," Michael chided her playfully. "Let's go, we're running late."

Michael led Carla back towards the door. Lifting his glass Nathan took a couple of mouthfuls and followed them. He winked at the group staring in silence at the sight of Carla being whisked off by a dark stranger with a soft Irish accent. Richard pursed his lips, put out. Camilla brought her glass down hard on the table. Patricia looked down embarrassed. At her feet was a large pink bag full of neatly wrapped parcels, all addressed to Carla.

Once they were outside Michael took his arm from around Carla's shoulder.

"I hope you didn't mind me butting in," he said unsure of the reaction he was going to get.

"No ... thanks." Carla was staring blankly, stunned. She had been so determined to get on with her new life it was a shock to see her old life still playing out right in front of her. But she was the outsider, shut out, usurped by a parasitic bimbo. If she was surprised by the ease with which her friends and neighbours had welcomed Camilla into their

92

cosy group after years of nurturing those friendships, the sight of Patricia and Brian signing up to their little soirees made her blood run cold.

"Sorry Carla," Jenny puffed. "The cat threw up."

Jenny clocked Michael and Nathan. "Hi, you coming in?"

"Actually, we're all leaving," said Michael.

"They're not fully booked, surely?" Jenny asked Carla. She thought Carla looked a little dazed. Maybe it was the realisation that her thirties were gone –for good.

"I'll explain later," said Carla.

"But it's your birthday. The Big Four O. We have to celebrate," urged Jenny.

"Don't remind me. Maybe I should go home."

"Your birthday?" echoed Michael. "Then you're not allowed to go home," he said firmly.

The Students Union was decorated with coloured fairy lights. Music pulsated over the hum of voices. Michael handed a student with long dark hair a ten pound note. The student pointed to a tray of drinks as he stamped four hands.

"The first drink is free. Help yourselves."

Carla looked around. The room was full of twenty somethings in denim shorts and vest tops. Carla picked up an orange juice in a white plastic cup. Jenny looked at her.

"I'm driving," Carla insisted.

Jenny picked up two plastic cups half filled with a dark red liquid and downed one of them.

"I'm not," she giggled.

The four of them stood awkwardly watching the dancers moving to a tuneless pulse. Michael began to think he'd made a bad choice.

"Are you familiar with this …" he searched for the right word.

"Music?" Carla supplied.

They burst out laughing.

"And now it's back to the eighties with Los Lobos and La Bamba," announced the DJ breaking through the drone. "Student grants and dodgy haircuts. Happy days."

A feel good guitar rift filled the room. Michael handed his drink to Nathan. Jenny grabbed Carla's orange juice. Michael led Carla onto the dance floor aided by a not so gentle poke in the back by Jenny, who sensed she was about to resist. Michael weaved through couples struggling to coordinate their shoulders and hips to the sway of the Latin beat.

"We have a saying in Ireland. If you dance on the day of a new decade, you'll dance your way through the next ten years."

"Do you really?" Carla ventured a hip wiggle.

They stood in a jostle free space facing each other.

"No," said Michael with a glint in his eye. "But it's worth a try."

Suddenly Michael's arm was around Carla's waist.

"Salsa is basically a rocking movement."

Carla felt the warmth of his breath on her ear. A tingle ran down her spine.

"Just follow me," Michael coaxed.

"Sorry," apologised Carla, treading on his toes.

Around them, the students were throwing each other into drunken spins.

"Just relax." Michael pulled her closer.

Carla's legs were turning to jelly, but somehow she managed to synchronise with Michael and even started to enjoy herself. Without warning La Bamba melted seamlessly into the sensuous sax riff of Careless Whisper.

Caught in mid spin, Michael and Carla burst our laughing. The seductive wail of the sax wrapped itself around them. Their eyes locked. Carla caught her breath.

"Curry?" Jenny popped up between them. "I'm starving."

"Me too," agreed Carla stepping away from Michael and regaining the strength in her legs.

"Great idea," agreed Michael, allowing the women to lead the way.

Nathan handed Michael back his drink.

"I haven't seen you move like in years," he smirked.

"It's been a while," smiled Michael.

He downed his drink and followed Carla and Jenny out of the building.

It was only just starting to get dark when Carla found a parking place around Queen Square. Carla pulled down the visor and checked her lipstick.

"You look gorgeous. Now, hurry up, I'm starving." slurred Jenny.

It was a short walk to the Indian restaurant. The fragrant smell of herbs and spices reached them on the warm summer breeze as they reached The Eastern Eye. A small balding man with a wide smile met them at the door and led them upstairs to a round table in a softly lit corner of the large room. The menu was packed with so many delicious choices so they decided to share a range of dishes. Jenny made of point of telling the smiley man Carla was celebrating a special birthday, and he brought them lots tantalising tasters.

Michael and Nathan reminisced about their time at university together, teasing each other over mullet haircuts, powder blue jeans and Old Spice aftershave.

Carla found herself sneaking glances at Michael, taking in his warm brown eyes and his lovely strong face. He caught her several times, smiled, and quickly looked away. Most of the two bottles of wine they had ordered ended up in Jenny's glass. By the end of the evening the tip of her nose glowed crimson. Stuffed, they rose to leave. Jenny leaned at a dangerous angle. Nathan tried to catch her before she hit the floor. He missed.

With her arms around the men's necks, Jenny dragged herself to Carla's car. Carla opened the rear door. The men lifted Jenny and slid her, head first, onto the back seat where she lay motionless. She began to snore. Carla slammed the door. Jenny jumped then curled up into a tight ball.

"Will you be alright getting her home?" asked Michael.

Carla laughed. "She can stay with me tonight. I'll put her in Bella's room."

"We'll be off then," said Michael reluctantly.

"Thank you for saving me from the smug marrieds club earlier, and for making my birthday so …"

"Memorable?" supplied Nathan.

"Special, … and memorable."

Nathan gave Carla a bear hug. Michael kissed her on the cheek. His dark stubble brushed her skin sending a second shiver down her back.

"Take care Carla," he said closing the car door after her.

The engine rumbled in harmony with Jenny's snoring. Carla pulled away from the kerb and waved to the figures in her rear view mirror. She smiled to herself. If someone had told her ten years ago that this was how she would have spent her fortieth birthday she'd have thought they were insane. But it was fine. She stroked her cheek. It was more than fine.

*****

Carla added lots of hot milk and a generous teaspoon of brown sugar to her black coffee. She breathed in the aroma. Why was the smell of coffee always better than the taste?

Cuddled up to the large panda that lived on Isabella's bed, Jenny was still in blissful reverie when Carla had popped her head around the door some fifteen minutes before.

They had got home just after midnight. Carla had led Jenny up the stairs, undressed her, and tucked her in.

Minutes later, curled up in her own bed, Carla had felt like she was floating on a cloud, and soon drifted off to sleep.

In the mirror that morning she'd noticed an unusual brightness to her skin. She felt positively serene. Was this life beginning at forty?

"Good night last night." Jenny stood in the doorway fully dressed. Apart from appearing a little dishevelled, she didn't look the least bit hung-over. "Thanks for putting me up."

"How's your head?" Carla poured black coffee into a large mug.

"I'm a rare specimen. I can drink like a fish, and the next day, nothing, right as rain," said Jenny cheerfully. A glint appeared in her eye, "did you enjoy your dance last night?"

"Coffee?" offered Carla evasively, handing her the mug and suppressing an urge to smile at the memory of Michael's arm around her waist and his warm breath in her ear.

Jenny took a couple of gulps of coffee. Fortified, she handed the mug back to Carla. "Right. Must go and check on the cat. I'll see myself out." She kissed Carla on the cheek.

"Happy birthday."

"Thanks for the lilies." Carla nodded at the bouquet that had arrived the previous afternoon.

With a wink, Jenny skipped down the hall humming La Bamba.

Hugging her mug with both hands, Carla took a sip and smiled to herself. The front door clicked shut. Carla took a crystal vase from the cupboard overhead and filled it with water. She unwrapped the bouquet. The distinct smell of lilies filled the kitchen. Stems trimmed, Carla began arranging the flowers.

DRING! Carla started, then rolled her eyes. What had Jenny left behind?

"Forgotten something?" said Carla opening the front door.

In front of her stood Patricia holding a pink bag of gift-wrapped parcels.

"Oh, it's you," said Carla coldly.

She didn't want any reminders of how her fortieth birthday celebrations had started, and especially of the betrayal by her best friend.

"Carla ..."

The door slammed shut. Carla had no intention of listening to a load of crap. She had the right to rebuild her life without the shadows of painful memories.

"Carla, let me explain," urged Patricia from the other side of the door.

"Go back to the dark side."

"Carla, this is childish. Please, just let me in."

Poking her tongue out at the back of the door Carla stomped back to the kitchen.

The scent of lilies had filled the room. She inhaled deeply to soothe her nerves, and tinkered with her flower arrangement, singing La Bamba at the top of her voice to block out any thoughts of her ex friend.

Carla sang her way up to a crescendo, hips wiggling.

"La ba-"

"Still keep your back door unlocked," came a voice from behind.

Carla's heart skipped a beat. She let out a shriek.

"Christ!" yelled Carla turning to face Patricia, "you nearly gave me a bloody heart attack."

Before Carla had the chance to regain her composure Patricia jumped in.

"Last night, I assumed you'd been invited. I brought your presents along," she said holding out the shiny bag. "I swear I had no idea that the gruesome twosome had been invited. There's no way I wouldn't see you on birthday. I expected you to be there."

Carla ignored the bag. "I'm the social leper remember," she spat. "How the hell does that work? I haven't stolen anybody's husband."

"It's their husbands they don't trust Carla," pacified Patricia. "Half the men sitting around that table have been inside another woman's knickers."

"But I'd never ..." protested Carla.

"That not the point. If it can happen to you, it can certainly happen to them. And that's a compliment," Patricia added.

"It doesn't feel like one," said Carla, half sighing, half smiling, relieved she hadn't lost her friend.

"Happy birthday." Patricia handed Carla her gifts.

"Thanks." Carla accepted the bag and gave Patricia a hug.

"Right," said Patricia her eyes lighting up, "who was that gorgeous man? You should have seen Chlamydia after you'd gone. She had a face like a slapped arse."

"Tell me something I don't know," chortled Carla.

DRING, interrupted the doorbell.

"I'll get rid of them," said Carla "and you can fill me in on the gossip."

Carla tripped down the hallway. Patricia fiddled with Carla's flower arrangement. As she stepped back to admire the lilies, Carla returned. Behind her was the handsome man from the pub.

"Oh, hello," smiled Patricia "we were just ..."

Carla coughed loudly.

"I'm not interrupting anything?" asked Michael, wondering why women always came in pairs.

"Not at all," replied Patricia a little too quickly, "in fact I was just leaving, right this minute."

Patricia sidled past them towards the hallway and flashed Carla a knowing smile. Carla's brows furrowed as a warning to Patricia to shut up.

Patricia held out her hand. "Nice to meet you ..."

"Michael." He shook her hand.

"Patricia."

Patricia blew Carla a kiss. "Call you later," she said with a wink.

In the corner of the kitchen Lellow cheeped excitedly at all the comings and goings. Michael walked over to take a closer look. His back turned, Patricia mouthed "hot" and fanned her face with her hand. Carla glared at her to get going. With a girlish giggle Patricia closed the front door behind her. Carla exhaled, relieved. Luckily Michael was deep in conversation with Lellow. Michael whistled and Lellow chirped, bouncing up and down on her perch.

"She's normally quite ... normal," said Carla. She was feeling a little dazed. Mornings were usually a lot quieter.

"Isn't she--?" asked Michael, recognising Patricia from the group in the pub the night before.

"Yes," confirmed Carla. "A misunderstanding. It's all sorted."

"Good," said Michael catching sight of the lilies.

"Nice flowers," he observed.

"From Jenny." Did Carla detect a note of jealousy?

"Good. I mean, they're very nice."

He offered Carla the rectangular package he was holding.

"Not flowers I'm afraid," he said shyly.

Carla giggled. "So I see."

"I hope you enjoy it."

Carla pulled away the sellotape and unwrapped the package.

"Caryl Churchill," she said reading the cover of the collection of plays. "Thank you. I saw *Top Girls* when Bella did it at school but I don't know any of her other plays."

"We'll be studying feminist theatre next semester," Michael gabbled, trying to hide his nervousness. "Not that I'm calling you a feminist. Nobody seems to want to be called that these days. I just thought she might be quite inspirational, you know, a major dramatist, a successful working mother. Not that I think- "

Carla put her hand over her mouth to stifle a giggle. Michael was out of his comfort zone and she didn't want to make it worse.

"Crap! I'm lecturing you." His face flushed with embarrassment. "I should have bought you flowers, chocolates or perfume. What kind of idiot buys a woman he really likes a book for her birthday?"

Realising what he had just said Michael ran his hand through his thick dark hair to hide his awkwardness. Carla noticed the flecks of grey. She thought they made him even more handsome.

Carla tried to stop herself grinning. "Did you just say you really like me?"

Michael shook his head. "I'm no good at this and, you're a student. It's awkward. I'm sorry. I never meant for this to come out."

"But you said you really like me?" Carla's stomach was filling with overactive butterflies.

"Yes." Michael took a deep breath and composed himself. "I promise I'll never mention it again."

"It's certainly awkward with me being a student," agreed Carla. She tried to sound serious but there was a mischievous glint in her eye. Maybe life really did begin at forty.

Michael crumpled slightly and studied Carla's kitchen floor. Carla put her hand on the back of Michael's neck. He stopped concentrating on the floor and looked into her eyes. Slipping his arm around her waist he kissed her gently on the lips. After a brief moment Carla pulled away. Michael panicked. Had he misread the signals?

"So we should definitely keep it quiet," she whispered, kissing his ear.

Relieved, Michael kissed Carla deeply on the mouth. His generous lips were soft and his tongue darted teasingly inside her mouth.

"Mmmm," she responded to what had to be the most erotic kiss ever.

Every nerve in her body was on a high state of alert. Michael's hand ran up and down Carla's back as Michael pulled her in tightly. Smoothly it then slipped across her waist and up to her breast.

"Where's the bedroom?" he murmured barley losing contact with her mouth.

Carla titled her head back. "You're full of surprises Professor."

She took his hand and led him through the door. They headed up the stairs, Michael behind Carla, kissing her neck. In the bedroom Michael scooped Carla up and put her gently on the bed. A flurry of fingers frantically searched for buttons, buckles, and zips. The last piece of clothing was unhooked and Carla's bra flew across the room. *Thank God for the Brazilian.* She owed her waxer a large tip. Michael's mouth worked down toward Carla's breasts. Running her hands through his hair she opened her eyes lazily. They widened in horror at the scene on the other side of her bedroom window. A yellow hot air balloon seemed to fill it. Several tourists were cheering and taking photographs of their unexpected landmark.

"Duck!" she yelled.

Finding strength she didn't know she had, Carla rolled Michael off the bed onto the floor under the window. With a slap she landed on top of him. Even a Brazilian couldn't make her feel sexy now.

"If you'd wanted to be on top, you only had to say," said Michael bemused.

"Look," said Carla, hoarse with shock and pointing up towards the window.

Michael lifted his head and glimpsed the balloon as it floated away.

The corners of Michael's mouth were twitching. There was a burst of relived laughter. Michael put his hand on the back of Carla's head drew her face close to his.

"Looks like our secrets out."

He kissed Carla passionately.

"Do you mind if I stay on top?" whispered Carla in his ear.

Michael put his hand onto the small of Carla's back and pressed her body closer. *Evidently not.*

*****

A week later, from her living room window, Carla watched Nellie's red mini park up outside her house. It was a beautiful sunny day. Dusky pink grandma's caps edged the front lawn bobbing in the breeze, and the lavender under the bay window released its soothing aroma. Carla breathed it in, not that she needed soothing these days. It had been a glorious week of lazy lunches in the garden with Michael. Afterwards they'd go upstairs and make love – with the curtains drawn! Despite their initial public display of affection, they kept a low profile. Thankfully the airborne voyeurs had kept the photographs for their personal entertainment, noted a relieved Carla as she checked The Bath Chronicle for evidence of the balloon incident that week.

Carla ran down her front path. By the time she reached her garden gate Isabella was out of the car and giving her mother a big hug.

"It's been the best year ever."

"I think you could be right," said Carla smiling to herself.

Putting her arms around the two girls Carla led them to the house.

"I hope you two are hungry ..."

"Starving," Nellie jumped in.

"Good, Gianni brought over a huge tray of lasagne last night and it's just begging to be eaten."

Isabella and Nellie made a big dent in the lasagne. They may have been built like willows but they had appetites like elephants. Full of enthusiasm for their time at Goldsmith's, they chirped away endlessly about Sylvia Plath, Homer and late night clubbing. Carla didn't feel in a position to warn them about the dangers of being up all night, she'd managed to slip in one or two all nighters herself, thanks to Patricia having Robbie sleep over. Instead she shooed them out onto the swing seat in the back garden while she prepared full strength espressos. By the time she carried the tray out into the garden both girls were fast asleep.

Returning to the kitchen, Carla put down the tray and made her way up to her bedroom. She had a little sleep of her own to catch up on.

After two days of rearranging her bedroom and catching up on proper food, Isabella and Nellie headed off to Glastonbury with a group of old school friends. With Robbie still seeing out the summer term, Carla and Michael were free to go on their first cycling date. Carla regarded cycling on the road as dancing with death, but she loved the Kennet and Avon canal towpath, especially the stretch from the Dundas Aqueduct to her favourite canal café in Bradford on Avon. They had cycled along it many times as a family. Carla knew she had to create new memories in familiar places. She understood now why old friends who had gone through marriage break ups had moved away. Being haunted by ghosts from the past made it hard to move on. But Carla loved living near her family and friends, and she loved Bath, so if there were any demons hiding behind familiar corners then she had no choice but to face, and banish them.

The wheels of Carla's green bicycle chattered like crickets as the tyres crunched over the gravel, muffling the birdsong and the distant rush of water. Being a weekday the path was almost empty, so Michael rode alongside her. The slow clunking of the barges and the calm reflections on the water were soporific. The smell of a barbecue breezed in through Carla's nose and tantalized her tongue. Ducks rested on the grassy bank on the water's edge. There wasn't a demon in sight.

The path veered to the right. Here the grass verge was wide. There was a bench in the centre of it. Michael rode towards the bench and dismounted. Carla followed.

"I never had you down as a lightweight," Carla teased.

Michael took a swig of his water bottle then held it out of Carla's reach.

"I take it you're not thirsty then?"

"Give it here." Carla bounced around trying to snatch the bottle as Michael pulled it out of her grasp.

"You'll have to earn it first." Michael gripped Carla by the waist with his free hand and pulled her towards him.

"Oh, I'm happy to earn my keep," she murmured her lips almost touching his.

Michael closed his eyes. Carla snatched the bottle and ran away squirting the water into her mouth and trying not to choke with laughter.

Michael caught her. "Pay up or else."

"Or else?" Carla giggled.

Michael put his hand on the back of Carla's neck, and kissed her.

A couple of barges drifted past.

"I forgot to tell you," whispered Carla as she nuzzled into Michael's neck, "Patricia's hiring a boat on Sunday. Brian is a barbecue legend. Do you fancy it?"

Michael dotted kisses around Carla's ears.

"I'd love to," he murmured, "but I'm not around on Sunday."

The traces of diesel that hung in the air stung Carla's nostrils.

"Oh."

Michael put one hand on Carla's shoulder and stroked the hair around her face with the other.

"I'm going back to Ireland for a couple of weeks. My father has just had a hip replacement. He's normally on his allotment all day, and now he's stuck at home driving my mother mad."

"When are you leaving?" Carla didn't expect to feel so unsettled, but family was family and she didn't want to get in the way.

"Tomorrow." Michael was hesitant. "I was going to tell you later."

"Well, with Bella home and Robbie about to break up for the summer, I won't have any time for you anyway," teased Carla getting on her bike.

"Then we'd better make the most of the time we've got left." Michael gripped his handlebars. He was relieved Carla had taken the news well.

Carla tossed her hair and pedalled towards the path.

"You'll have to catch me first."

*****

Chapter Six

Four weeks went by before Michael returned. He had emailed Carla almost every day with bulletins on the progress of prize-winning vegetables and the battle against insect invasions. He seemed to be enjoying his mother's Sunday roasts and being pampered. Carla was more than happy to leave that side of things to his mammy. After twenty years of looking after Richard's every need she was glad of the break. Without the pressure of coursework and exams she was free to devote her time to taking Robbie to his activities, and spending girlie time with Isabella. Their shopping trips were always fruitful. Isabella had a knack of spotting an unusual skirt or top that would suit Carla perfectly. The buzz generated by retail therapy was then prolonged with a visit to the deli for a fully caffeinated cappuccino, a large slice of mille foglie, and a catch up with Angela, Gianni and Mamma about their plans to give the deli a makeover. The deli was going to get a fresh coat of paint, the floor would be revarnished and a wall would be dedicated to Gianni's growing collection of artwork aimed at tourists, featuring landmarks like the Royal Crescent and the Roman Baths.

Then, when Isabella found a job in a boutique, and Robbie enrolled on a cricket course, Carla set about giving her kitchen a makeover. Inspired by Lellows soft yellow feathers she decided to replace the dull biscuit colour with the colour of sunshine.

Dressed in an old pair of shorts and vest top, Carla applied the sodden roller, to the final section of wall. Her olive skin, now a golden brown, was sprayed with yellow freckles. The latest hit from the reunited Take That played on the radio. Carla rolled the paint onto the wall swinging her hips in time to the song and wailing the occasional word. Michael's last email said he would be back the following evening so tonight was for pampering and preening; a luxurious bubble bath, skin massaged from top to toe with her favourite lavender body lotion, and nails cut and polished. Butterflies fluttered in her stomach at the thought of seeing him. She put down the roller and picked up a small brush to fill in the gaps in the corner of the wall. A pair of arms gripped her around the waist. Carla breathed in sharply.

"You should really keep your front door closed, you never know who might wander in."

Carla turned and faced the voice.

"I thought you weren't back until tomorrow," she beamed, covering Michael's face with kisses.

"Missed me then?" Michael said, drawing her in closer.

"Not at all," said Carla dabbing the end of Michael's nose with the paintbrush.

Dipping his finger in the pot of yellow gloop, Michael put a yellow dot on each of Carla's cheeks. As she lifted the paintbrush to retaliate he grabbed it and threw it on the dustsheet. Before Carla could react she was hanging over Michael's shoulder giggling helplessly. He took her through the hallway, closed and bolted the front door and carried her upstairs.

Michael made a couple more short trips back to Ireland that summer. He joked it was just to make sure his parents' marriage survived as long as his father's new hip. Isabella went back to her flat in London at the beginning of September. Robbie, having spent the summer playing cricket and seemingly growing six inches in as many weeks, returned to school looking like a young man. Carla had managed to avoid any contact with Richard. He would leave messages on the answerphone letting Robbie know when he was coming to pick him up. Carla winced at the sound of his phoney chirpiness, but it was better than talking to him.

Jenny had been in San Francisco all summer with Martin's parents. They were glad to share memories of their only son with someone who loved him as dearly as them.

Carla finally caught up with her in the library at the start of the semester.

"All summer? Seriously? You kept that quiet." Jenny faced Carla across one of the study table, eyes wide with disbelief, and with more than a hint of excitement.

"That's the idea," whispered Carla, "I don't want it broadcast all over campus."

An earnest looking young man surrounded by a pile of books on the table next to them peered over his rimless round glasses catching Carla's eye. He pointed at a sign on the wall. Quiet Study Area.

"Sorry," Carla mouthed.

She looked down at her note pad, tried to look as though she was writing something significant, and drew a heart.

"I can't imagine being with anyone else after Martin," whispered Jenny.

The time she had spent with Martin's parents had made her feel close to him again. Over the last year she felt he had been slipping away, and it frightened her. He was the last thing she thought about at night and the first when she woke up, and that was the way she wanted it. She owed him that.

"Things change Jen, whether we want them to or not," said Carla gently.

A loud cough. The young man gave them a withering look. Like two naughty schoolgirls they pretended to make notes.

"You're probably going to say no," whispered Jenny.

Intrigued, Carla put down her pen.

"You know you're really good at directing our exam pieces ..."

Carla knew this was a gross exaggeration. She just offered the occasional suggestion just like everyone else.

"Where's this going?" Carla eyed Jenny with mock suspicion, but hadn't a clue what was coming next.

Jenny put on her pleading face.

"We really need someone to assist our director on The Rondo's production of *Pygmalion*."

Jenny let the words hang in the air, expecting Carla to start going on about how busy she was. Carla felt a tingle of excitement run down her spine.

"You never said you were doing *Pygmalion*. I'd love to."

"You would?" spluttered Jenny.

"Yes."

"Fantastic. We have a rehearsal tonight."

A pencil snapped. Ernest student glared at them.

"Coffee?" suggested Jenny, sensing it might be a good time to leave.

"Love one."

Carla leaned towards the student who was making detailed diagrams with his pencil stub.

"There's more to life than studying you know. You want to get out there and get some life experience."

Jenny stifled a giggle. Assisting the director on *Pygmalion* would certainly be one of life's experiences. But Carla would discover that for herself.

Just before eight that evening Nathan met Carla and Jenny inside the auditorium. Carla detected a twinkle in his eye. *So, Michael has told him about us.*

"Our new assistant director," said Nathan with an uncharacteristic flourish. "Welcome."

The word "new" jarred.

"New? What happened to the old one?" asked Carla.

Jenny threw Nathan a warning glance. Nathan coughed to give himself time to think.

"Just a figure of speech. Welcome, our only assistant director." He trailed off unconvincingly.

Jenny glared at him. Mouth firmly shut, Nathan lead them to the stage. Carla began to feel nervous. On the stage stood a timid looking young woman in her early twenties. A skinny man in his fifties with a deeply lined face and wavy grey hair reached into the inside pocket of a battered leather jacket hanging over a chair. In a split second the man had taken a swig from a hip flask and put it back in the jacket pocket. He swiftly turned his attention to the girl.

"Eliza Doolittle is an East End flower girl, not the fifth member of the Beatles," he spat in a show of exasperation.

The girl looked as if she was about to burst into tears. Why was Quentin talking about beetles? Carla looked at Jenny alarmed.

"His bark is worse than his bite, you'll see."

Carla wasn't convinced she wanted to see any more. As they walked down the side isle towards the stage Quentin's cold blue eyes fixed on Jenny.

"Good of you to turn up," he said in a nasal voice.

His focus shifted to Carla. The eyes turned to ice.

"And what have we here? Another escapee from care in the community?"

Carla flinched. She wanted to turn around and run out. Nathan stepped forward.

"This is Carla. She has very kindly agreed to be your assistant."

Automatically Carla held out a shaky hand.

"Pleased to ..."

Ignoring her hand Quentin spun to face the empty tiers of red seats.

"Really," he said with mock surprise in an aside the empty stalls.

He took a step towards Carla, who thought he was about to throw her out.

"Well, your first job," he said slowly, as if addressing an imbecile, "is to try and get our leading lady here to ..." He turned his leading lady and continued in an East End accent "soun' laeek Eelaeeza Dooli'le."

Quentin shoved his copy of the play at Carla. She scrambled to catch it. *Mental note. Kill Jenny later.*

"I need a drink," announced Quentin as he picked up his jacket and slithered in the direction of the bar.

Nathan smiled at Carla apologetically and followed Quentin. Best keep on eye on his bar stock.

"Jen, I'm not sure this is a good idea," whispered Carla.

A timid voice cut in. "I could really do with some help."

Eliza Doolittle was about the same age as Isabella, and Carla could see by the look of trepidation in her eyes she needed support. It was impossible for Carla to say no. In a similar situation she hoped someone would be there for her own daughter. Carla opened the book. Jenny sneaked a wink at Laura who was now smiling with relief.

Over at the bar Quentin perched on a tall stool.

"A double of your finest Irish," he demanded.

Silently, Nathan placed a glass under the optic and drew the honey coloured liquid. He was tired and didn't want to get drawn into a conversation about Quentin's finest hour as a freelance theatre director in London. The whiskey glass explained why Quentin's finest hour was long gone, and why he now complained about being stuck in local theatre wasting his expertise.

A loud ring broke the silence.

"Excuse me." Nathan placed the glass in front of Quentin and withdrew into the office behind the bar.

Quentin picked up the glass and downed the whiskey in one. He looked around scornfully. Those talentless women on the stage were wasting their time attempting to do justice to the genius that was Shaw, and that spineless so called Theatre Director couldn't direct himself out of a paper bag. Slinking to the other side of the bar, Quentin pulled the hipflask out of his pocket, unscrewed the top and held it under the whiskey optic until he had drained the contents into his flask. Taking a couple of large gulps from his flask he walked unsteadily towards the stage area.

"Ow, eez ye-ooa san, is ee?" said Laura in her improved East End accent.

Carla was pleased she could at last put to good use all the evenings she spent stuck at home with nothing better to do than watch East Enders while Richard was busy "working".

"That's really good Laura," encouraged Carla.

"Your accent is at least beginning to crawl down the M6," hissed Quentin. "We must be grateful for small mercies."

The three women froze. They had been having so much fun on their own they had forgotten who was in charge. A bony hand flicked out and snatched the play off Carla. Behind Quentin's back Jenny gave Carla a thumbs up, desperate for her to stay. But Carla had already decided that if she survived the rest of the evening, she wasn't coming back for more abuse from this pickled string of gristle.

"Right, the scene where Mrs. Pierce takes Eliza up to her room," commanded Quentin.

Jenny and Laura flicked frantically through their book. A malicious smile crossed Quentin's face.

"Off book," he said slowly, anticipating pleasure from Jenny's and Laura's reactions.

They looked up, confused.

"You said off book by next week," ventured Jenny.

Laura nodded nervously.

"I said no such thing." The corners of Quentin's mouth curled slyly, like a cobra about to pounce on its victim. "Amateurs," he declared, staggering around and waving his arms at the empty stalls. "Nothing but a bunch of amateurs."

That was it. Carla had had enough. She picked up her jacket. Jenny glared at Quentin who was still gesticulating and muttering insults. In frustration she kicked a parasol that was lying on the floor. It glided in slow motion across the stage stopping directly under Quentin's right foot as he stamped in mid tirade. He trod on the parasol. It slid out from under him. Already unsteady from the shots of whiskey, Quentin lost his balance and fell backwards. The women stared, waiting for him to jump up suddenly and continue his attack with renewed ferocity. Realising that

Quentin wasn't going to spring back into life, Carla rushed over to him. Gingerly she prised open his left eye. The bloodshot eyeball rolled around. Alcohol fumes from Quentin's breath choked her. With a look of disgust, she fanned them away. *Thank God he's still breathing.* She looked up at Jenny who stood beside her.

"What did you do that for?" Carla's eyes flashed angrily.

Jenny knelt beside Quentin's corpse.

"It was an accident," replied Jenny leaning forwards to take a closer look. Her head jerked back as if she'd inhaled a dose of smelling salts.

"Christ, he's pissed. Lets get him out of the way so he can sleep it off." Jenny grabbed one of Quentin's arms and signalled to Laura to grab the other. "With any luck he won't remember a thing."

"We can always tell him he fell asleep," said Laura lamely as she helped Jenny drag Quentin's limp body towards the empty seats.

Grabbing Quentin by the lapels Carla helped Jenny and Laura hoist him up into a seat.

"He's going to have a lump on the back of his head the size of a tennis ball."

"He's anaesthetised. He won't feel a thing," said Jenny confidently.

She took a Sherlock Holmes hat from a cardboard box on the floor and placed it carefully on Quentin's lolling head. Then she pulled out a long curved pipe.

"What the hell are you doing?" asked Carla.

Worried that Quentin might somehow hear her, Laura stifled a giggle. Jenny deftly climbed over to the row of seats behind and manipulated Quentin's lowered jaw.

"It's elementary my dear Watson." Jenny imitated Quentin's nasal hiss. "Nothing but a bunch of amateurs.

She stuck the pipe in his mouth and clamped his jaw shut. In spite of herself Carla smiled. Seizing Carla's moment of weakness Jenny winked at her.

"Now, what about that scene? You won't mind filling in until our director regains consciousness will you?"

Laura gave Carla pleading look. Quentin started to snore peacefully.

"Do I have a choice?" asked Carla picking up the play from the floor.

Without the fear instilled by Quentin's bullying, the actors relaxed into their roles. Carla had a knack of suggesting small manageable changes that gradually improved the scenes between Laura's Eliza and Jenny's motherly Mrs Pearce. Jenny would have made a lovely mother thought Carla as her pen hovered over her note pad, but sadly it looked like that boat had sailed.

"Ah—oo! Ah—oo!" squealed Eliza sitting in the large cardboard box which doubled as a bath. Her East End accent had come on in leaps and bounds in the last hour.

Mrs Pierce picked up the long handled wooden back brush. An occasional snort reminded Carla that they still had to deal with Quentin when he woke up. There was a sly smile on his face as if he was dreaming up a new scene of humiliation for his petrified actors. Maybe he'd still be asleep when they were finished, then they could leave him to Nathan reasoned Carla hopefully.

Mrs Pierce got stuck in, scrubbing Eliza Dolittle with the back brush. A newly confident Laura let out a piercing scream.

Quentin's limp body jolted as if he'd been shot. The pipe, which had been resting precariously on his bottom lip, clattered onto the floor. Arms flailing, a dazed Quentin tried to work out where he was. Then he focused on Jenny with a look that might turn her to stone. The three women stared at the viper as he scanned the scene. Turning puce with anger, Quentin stood unsteadily. He put his hand on his throbbing head, looked momentarily confused, then pulled off the Sherlock Holmes hat and threw it at Jenny. The women backed away unsure of what Quentin might do. They secretly hoped he would pass out again so they could escape.

"You!" he spat pointing a crooked finger at Jenny, "you, tried to kill me."

Jenny shook her head innocently. Fumbling in his jacket pocket, Quentin pulled out his phone with a large theatrical gesture. He waved it in front to Jenny.

"I'm going to get you locked up for GBH," he snarled with a devilish look in his eye.

"It was an accident," Jenny blurted.

"Liar!" roared Quentin.

He made a fumbled attempt to dial.

"If you make that call, I'll report you for stealing from the bar."

Nathan stood behind Quentin holding the empty whisky bottle.

"How dare you insinuate ..."

"I'm not insinuating anything," Nathan cut in firmly, "I can smell your breath from the other end of the theatre. Planning to drive home were you? Go ahead call the Police."

Quentin made a dramatic sweeping gesture with his arm and nearly toppled over.

"I refuse to prostitute my artistic integrity a moment longer. See how you manage without me. Damn you all."

He attempted to walk away majestically, but inebriated and concussed, Quentin meandered past the bar, and eventually reached the door.

Laura suppressed a nervous giggle. Jenny was relieved to avoid being arrested for attempted murder, and Carla wondered why she had agreed to come to this mad house in the first place.

"Amateurs!"

The door slammed behind Quentin.

"Good riddance," muttered Jenny quietly, still fearful he might come back.

"Yes, but what are we going to do without a director?" asked Laura.

Nathan's eyes twinkled. He looked at Carla, who realised with horror all eyes were on her.

*****

Hair brushed and ready to go out, Carla switched off the bathroom light. How on earth had Nathan talked her into directing *Pygmalion*? Whatever the answer, she had left the theatre the previous evening committed to directing two months of rehearsals. Nathan had promised to take care of sets, costumes and publicity. Jenny had given her a big thank you hug. Carla wasn't sure whether to hug her back or thump her.

Tonight she had planned a quiet drink with Michael. Hopefully he would give her a few tips to stop her directing début being a total disaster.

Picking her handbag up off the floor, Carla popped her head around the living room door. Wrapped up like a hot dog, Robbie sat in his quilt watching Top Gear. Seeing Carla, he slipped his hot water bottle under his quilt.

"See you later, Sausage," said Carla.

Robbie gave her a pathetic smile.

"Are you alright? You look a bit flushed" Carla put her hand on Robbie's forehead.

"I'm a bit hot, but I'll be okay," said Robbie putting on his brave face.

Carla ran her hands through his thick hair.

"Mmm, are you sure?"

"Yes, really. You go out."

Carla hesitated. She stroked his cheek.

"You know what? I can go out another night."

"I don't want to …"

"You're not. Now, how about a big mug of tea with lots of honey?"

Robbie snuggled deeper into the quilt.

"Yes, please, and can I have some custard creams?"

Carla nodded smiling. Robbie was looking better already.

"Thanks mum. Oh, and can I have the tea in my giant mug?"

Steam puffed out of the kettle as the water rumbled inside. Carla held the phone to her ear with one hand and dropped a tea bag into Robbie's mug with the other.

"I'm sorry. Do you mind? It was the hot water bottle on the forehead trick. I was out last night. He just wants me home."

She picked up the kettle and poured boiling water over the teabag.

"Thanks. I'll ring you tomorrow."

Carla folded the Bath Chronicle. Apart from a punch up involving some of the Bath Rugby players at a city centre watering hole, the city was reassuringly tranquil. Robbie lay curled up on the sofa, laughing at Stephen Fry's game show repartee.

"How're you feeling?" asked Carla trying not to smirk.

"What?" Robbie eyes stayed glued to the television. "Oh yeah," he remembered, "bit better."

DRING! DRING! Carla jumped. Damn that bell.

"Should be made illegal," Carla muttered as she opened the door, expecting an energy sales rep.

"You look as though you're about to kill someone," laughed Michael. "Don't shoot. I come bearing gifts."

He held up a huge pizza box from Bianco's Mangia Bene, topped with smaller boxes, including a *James Bond* DVD. The unmistakeable aroma of Mamma's and Gianni's cooking made her salivate.

"I said it was for Robbie so they threw in a few extras."

"I haven't ..."

"It's all right. I told them I was your plumber."

118

"Really," laughed Carla, "In that case you'd better come in and fix my pipes."

Feeling apprehensive, Carla led Michael into the living room.

"Robbie, this is Michael, a friend of mine. He's bought pizza."

"Nonna's Pizza!" declared Robbie his eyes lighting up. "Get in."

Michael looked at Carla to translate. She winked.

"I'll get some plates."

The final credits rolled. Another 007 mission accomplished against the odds. Robbie yawned.

"Time for bed. You've got school in the morning."

Robbie dragged himself up still enveloped in the quilt. He was stuffed with the pizza, and ice-cream that Mamma Bianco had given *the plumber* for her grandson. A Bart Simpson hot water bottle slipped from inside the quilt and landed with a glug. Carla looked at Robbie and pressed her lips together to suppress a smile. He picked it up and shrugged his shoulders.

"Thanks for the video and the pizza."

Michael nodded, relieved that Carla's teenage son was easy-going and well mannered, unlike himself at that age.

"Night," said Robbie shuffling out of the room.

"Night."

With the sofa vacated Michael rose out of the armchair. He took Carla's hand and pulled her onto his lap. He squeezed Carla around the waist with one hand and put his beer to his lips with the other. Robbie's head reappeared around the door.

"If you two are going to have sex, make sure you use a condom."

Beer sprayed over the empty pizza box as Michael choked on his beer. Carla's mouth opened and closed like a fish.

119

"Have-have you given your father the same advice?" was all she could come up with.

"Don't have to. He's had a vasectomy."

The pizza box got another shower.

"Night." Robbie's head disappeared.

Carla and Michael stared at each other in silence until the slow thuds of Robbie's feet reached the top of the stairs.

"That came out of the blue," said Michael finally swallowing his beer.

"You're telling me. Richard's had the snip? I had no idea."

*****

Nathan held open the door of The Rondo Theatre as Carla ran towards him from the other side of the road.

"I thought you'd changed your mind," he said, relieved.

"Sorry I'm late, I had to drop Robbie off at a friends."

"They've learnt their lines and they're ready to go."

That's more than I am, thought Carla as she followed Nathan into the auditorium. "Great."

Following her introductions to Paul, the play's Professor Higgins, a quietly spoken fifty something with a thick head of grey, and Jim, small and flamboyant, in the role of Pickering, Carla asked the cast to run through Eliza's elocution lesson.

Paul's delivery was slow and wooden.

"A cappatee." Laura was relaxed and natural.

Jim bobbed up and down bursting to get to his line.

He bellowed out at the empty auditorium, both arms outstretched, and completely ignoring Miss Doolittle.

Carla wanted to bury her face in her hands. This man had played too many pantomime dames.

"Thank you. Let's just stop there a moment. Well done. You know your lines. Now I want to forget about the audience. Keep it real and the laughs will come naturally. Let's take a quick break."

Carla walked to the bar where Nathan was putting up posters. She slumped onto a stool.

"How's it going?"

"I can't do this." Carla's head was in her hands.

Nathan poured her a glass of white wine. Carla looked at the glass. With visions of turning into Quentin, she pushed it away.

"Give them a chance," said Nathan switching on the kettle. "I know it's not the National but they're really willing. Besides, there's another very good reason why I want you to keep going."

"You enjoy watching me suffer?" groaned Carla.

"I'm leaving the theatre." Nathan poured the boiled water into a mug.

Carla lifted her head.

"I've got a new job, with the Arts Council." He scooped the teabag out of the mug.

"When? Where?" The last thing Carla needed was to be left to run this play on her own.

"Not until the summer." Nathan stirred the strong brew. Just how Carla needed it.

"There's no need to panic." He handed her the tea. "So there's plenty of time for you to/"

Carla heart skipped a beat. "Me to what?"

"Get the experience you need to apply for my job," said Nathan calmly.

"That's impossible. I can't do your job. I'm a housewife-person-mother. I can't run a theatre."

Nathan put his hand on Carla's arm.

"Carla, you have far more to offer than you realise," he said as if tuned into a level of wisdom Carla had been denied access to.

Nathan nodded in the direction of the stage.

"Your cast is waiting."

Feeling slightly stunned, but strangely soothed by Nathan's calm assurance Carla made her way back to her cast.

"Okay, let's run that again, and remember ..."

"Keep it real," they chorused.

Half an hour later, Carla was starting to feel buoyed up by the slow by clear improvement. The actors forgot about acting and started to become their characters.

Michael slipped into the theatre unnoticed by Carla, who was engrossed in discussions with the actors about the beginning of Eliza's transformation from ladette to lady.

Nathan handed Michael a glass of locally brewed cider.

"How's she doing?" asked Michael, slightly bemused by Carla's gesticulating to the actors as she walked around the stage with a new air of confidence.

"She's got her work cut out, but she'll be fine."

Laura's line rang out with the clarity of an emerging lady. Carla gave Laura a thumbs-up, followed by a round of applause for the actors as she wound up the rehearsal. She felt relieved that her motley troupe appeared to be turning a corner. Maybe applying for Nathan's job wasn't such a bad idea after all.

*****

Grey matted clouds blocked the sunlight as Carla sat at her kitchen table trying to put together a covering letter. It needed to sound dynamic if it was going to support her application for the role of artistic director at The Rondo Theatre. When she led in bed drifting between sleep and consciousness she was the most articulate person on the planet. Beautifully structured sentences flowed into vibrant paragraphs, and her dreamtime speeches had hundreds applauding with gusto. Faced with a blank sheet of paper her brain froze. *Just write something. It's a bloody covering letter not a dissertation on lesbian feminist theatre.*

"Dear Sirs, My name is Carla Bianco. She scribbled it out. Sounding like a seven year old wouldn't get her the job.

"Dear Sirs, I hear there is…" More scribbling out. "Dear Sirs, I wonder if …" Carla threw the scrunched up sheet of paper on the floor. Time for a tea break. Steam curled up from the kettle spout. Like the mist hanging in mid air, Carla suspended her thoughts for a moment. Words drifted towards her. Sentences came fully formed. Five minutes later she drew a line under her name. First draft was complete. Fifteen minutes after that she crossed the road, to the post box. For a second she hesitated, the large envelope hovering over the gaping mouth. Carla crossed her fingers with one hand and let go of the envelope with the other. The soft clunk as it hit the bottom of the empty box filled her with a sense of satisfaction. Time for that cup of tea.

*****

Chapter Seven

Over the next couple of weeks Carla pushed aside the fear that the theatre committee would take one look at her application and throw it straight in the bin. With essays to write, a play to direct and Robbie to run around, life was more than busy. She really looked forward to Friday nights; date night. Michael and Carla steered clear of the city centre where they would be easily spotted by the large groups of students wandering in a merry haze through Bath's watering holes. Instead they drove out to country pubs in the outlying villages, where they felt free to be a normal couple.

Carla's alarm beeped annoyingly. She forced her eyelids apart.

"Robbie, get up," she shouted through the bedroom wall, "tennis in half an hour."

Robbie walked into Carla's bedroom looking smug. He was already in his kit and chewing on a piece of toast loaded with peanut butter.

"Alright clever clogs, go and play on your computer while I sort myself out."

Chuckling to himself, Robbie went into his bedroom. He seemed to grow taller everyday. His face was still fuzz free. Whilst Carla loved the feel of Michael's stubble on her cheeks she wanted Robbie to remain her smooth faced baby boy.

Bleary eyed, in an oversized T shirt, Carla thumped down the stairs. The mail plopped onto the tiles in the hallway.

"Bills, junk mail, more bills," Carla muttered to herself still half asleep. Then- a crisp white envelope. In a second all fuzziness evaporated. She dropped the rest of the pile on the floor, ripped the envelope apart and pulled out the single sheet. Eyes as wide a saucers, she read the short paragraph inviting her to attend and interview the following Wednesday.

"Y-e-e-s!" she yelled breaking into a victory jig.

*****

The other four candidates looked like they'd been plucked from opposite corners of the planet. The impossibly attractive woman in her early thirties with flawlessly applied black eyeliner, pillar box red lips, and porcelain skin could have been Deeta Von Teeze's younger sister. An earnest young man with short dark hair and glasses sat quietly reading. Carla squinted as she tried to make out the title of his book. Her eyes were definitely going. *Something about education and theatre.* Before she had time to panic over her lack of preparation, Nathan came out of the office.

"Carla, would you come through please," he said in professional mode, wearing a polite smile.

Feeling nervous, Carla walked past two other candidates, registering only blurred faces.

Nathan held open the office door.

"Please take a seat." He pointed at a single wooden chair facing a long trestle table.

By the time Carla had perched herself securely on the chair, Nathan was behind the long table flanked by a white haired woman and a thin faced man with glasses. She felt like she'd walked into an episode of The Apprentice.

Fortunately Nathan bore no resemblance to the grumpy gnome who usually graced the centre of that panel. He gave her a reassuring nod.

The white haired woman peered at Carla.

"I see from your application Ms Bianco that you have a fair amount of business experience."

"Yes, I've helped run the family business since my teens," replied Carla.

"Good," chipped in thin-faced man. "A lot of candidates fail to appreciate that this role requires business as well as creative skills. In addition to ticket sales a community theatre relies on it's bar takings and new ideas to keep it afloat. "

The butterflies in Carla's stomach began to subside.

"Do you have any ideas that might provide additional revenue?" asked the white haired woman.

"Er-er" stuttered Carla. Why hadn't Nathan told her they'd be expecting a business plan?

"Well, there are a lot of retired people in the area. We could put on tea dances and afternoon concerts to get full use out of the building," she ventured.

"Excellent." The man with glasses smiled.

Nathan gave Carla a tiny nod of approval. Inwardly she heaved a sigh of relief.

"Now let us look at your qualifications," said the white haired woman peering even more intently as she ran her eyes down Carla's C.V.

"I see you're still at university."

"I finish this summer," answered Carla. "I believe Nathan-er Mr McDonald will be here until then."

"You don't seem to have any previous theatrical experience," noted the glasses.

"Er-" Carla felt her short lived confidence drain away.

"Ms. Bianco is currently involved with our theatre as a new director," said Ian.

"I see," nodded the thin-faced man. Then we will have the pleasure of seeing your work first hand."

Carla forced a smile and tried not to look terrified.

"We have to be honest, as things stand you're not qualified for this post," said the woman.

Carla felt completely deflated. It was just as well Nathan had his head down making notes. He shouldn't have made her believe she would be taken seriously. She placed both feet firmly on the floor ready to get up.

"However," said the man, before Carla's backside parted company with the chair, "we are prepared to consider your application on condition that your directorial debut reaches the highest standards of community drama."

"And your reference from the university indicates you are on course to achieve a very good result in your degree, added the other half of the double act.

"Thank you," said Carla.

She felt like she'd been tap dancing of quicksand. An espresso was required, pronto.

126

Outside the theatre, the emission from a passing lorry made her splutter. Great. Carbon monoxide poisoning. What next?

"How did it go?"

Michael had crept up behind her.

"Christ, You nearly gave me heart attack."

Michael smiled. Carla was overdramatic at times.

"And it's not funny. I feel like I've just gone ten rounds with Mike Tyson."

"You wouldn't last one round," joked Michael, putting his hand on Carla's shoulder.

"I don't stand a chance."

"Of course you do. You're doing all the right things. Your studies, the play, it'll pay off. Trust me,"

"That's easy for you to say." Carla pushed Michael's hand away. He didn't know it was going to pay off. She felt suddenly angry. How dare he predict her future. He didn't know anything.

"What do you mean?" asked Michael taken aback by Carla's sudden attack.

"What I said. Easy for you to say from the comfort of your cosy academic world. In my world I need that job. In my world my ex husband keeps cutting the pathetic allowance I get to bring up our children, so he can throw it away on another holiday, and he gets away with it because he knows I can't afford to fight back."

Tears were streaming down Carla's face as she ran along the street. Talking about Richard to Michael, to anyone, was something she avoided. She had been left to get on with rebuilding her life. That meant drawing a line under the past, but the past had a habit of barging its way into her present.

A hand gripped her arm stopping Carla in her tracks. Michael looked straight into her eyes. He held her firmly to make sure she didn't take off again.

"I'm on your side. Remember?"

Feeling the tension subside from Carla's body Michael risked letting go of one arm. He stroked away Carla's tear with his fingertips, cupped her face and gently kissed her lips.

In that fuzzy world between sleep and waking, Carla felt Michael's arms wrapped around her body. He fitted perfectly around her. They were made to be together. It didn't matter that she wasn't going to get the job. She already had everything she wanted. Turning to face Michael, she snapped into consciousness. Carla was alone. A folded sheet of paper lay in the depression on the empty pillow. Carla grabbed it. In the split second it took to unfold the note her heart was already pounding.

Whatever you dream you can do. I hope you like your present. Michael. X.

Relief flooded Carla's body. She hugged the note to her chest. What present? At the foot of the bed lay a soft rectangular package. Normally Carla unwrapped presents carefully and dutifully recycled the paper, but anxious to see what Michael had given her she tore a ragged hole across the package. She held up a black T shirt. In white letters the words *Keep It Real* were printed across the back. Holding it up against her she could see it was a perfect fit, just like her and Michael.

*****

Carla faced her stage crew. They were camouflaged, from head to toe in black. She wore the T shirt Michael had given her. The last three weeks had been a blur of activity. With Nathan's guidance, she had sourced costumes and props, designed programmes, and put up posters in every shop and noticeboard that would take them.

It was six thirty. One hour till curtain up. Isabella, Robbie, Gianni, Angela, Mamma Bianco, Patricia, Nellie, and the twins stood in a semi circle on the stage. Carla tried to sound like she knew what she was doing.

"Lets make this a night to remember. Mamma, you're on teas and coffees. Stay away from the sherry, it doesn't mix with your tablets."

Mamma walked off with a *what do you know?* snort, and went in search of a small sherry to keep her going.

"Angela, you're front of house. If you're not selling enough tickets drag them in off the street."

"I'm on the case," said Angela lifting her skirt above her knee with a pout."

"She said attract people, not drive them away," teased Gianni.

Giving Gianni a swift slap across the back of the head Angela wiggled her way to the front of house.

"Isabella and Nellie, you're selling programmes," said Carla handing Isabella a cardboard box. "Gianni, great job on the scenery."

"Down to team work," said Gianni and gave Robbie, Alex and Sam a high five.

"Well team, it's time to go back stage with your stage manager. Patricia, you happy with the props?"

"All under control Miss," teased Patricia. "It's the black hole for us boys."

Patricia, Gianni and the boys were swallowed through the back curtain. Alone on the stage Carla felt queasy. This was where her job ended. It was like handing your child over to the teacher on the first day of school.

Thanks to a coachload of GCSE students, it was a full house. On stage Laura shone as Eliza.

As the play drew to a close, she delivered her lines with all the confidence she had lacked at that disastrous rehearsal with Quentin. The audience chuckled at pompous Professor

Higgins getting hit on the head by the pair of slippers Eliza threw at him. At the far end of the first row, busily making notes and whispering to each other, sat the man and woman who'd interviewed Carla. She sneaked a look. *At least they're smiling*, she thought. Michael squeezed Carla's hand. On Carla's other side sat Isabella, who smiled at the gesture. Carla held her breath as her directorial debut drew to a close. The cast had been magnificent, the audience warm and appreciative.

Blackout. A healthy burst of applause. Carla finally exhaled, woozy with relief. She'd done it. Surely she now stood as good a chance as anyone else of getting the artistic director's job. Before the clapping died down she slipped through the side door and up the narrow steps to the dressing room. The actors were on an adrenaline high. Carla threw her arms around each of them and popped the champagne that had been chilling in the fridge.

The bar was packed. As Carla made her way towards Michael, audience members congratulated her on her successful debut. Isabella ran down the central aisle and gave Carla a hug.

"You played a blinder tonight, Mum."

"I hope they think so," said Carla, with a nod towards the back of the auditorium where the adjudicators sat deep in conversation.

"I'm sure they were blown away," said Isabella.

She looked over at Michael and Nathan, who had been joined by glowing Jenny.

"He's nice. I like him."

"I like him too," replied Carla.

"It's good to see you happy." Isabella kissed her mother on the cheek. "Me and Nellie are taking the boys home. See you later."

Carla stood for a moment, taking everything in. Life was good. If she got the job it would be great. At least now she felt she had a fighting chance. She looked over at Michael as he chatted to Jenny and Nathan. He must have felt her eyes on him. He looked over at Carla, winked and gestured for her to join them.

"Congratulations."

A figure blocked her path. Richard stood in front of her. She hadn't seen him in over a year. When he came to pick Robbie up she made sure she was in the kitchen with the radio on, not even wanting to hear his voice. Carla noted that he'd put on a few pounds and was his hair loss was accelerating.

"What are you doing here?"

All those years of keeping him happy. Now she could be as blunt as she liked.

"Can I have a word?"

"It's not a good time. You can put the cheque in the post. Robbie's overdue some new clothes."

"It won't take long. Please it's important."

"Is everything okay?"

Michael stood next to Richard. He would have recognised Richard from the photographs in Robbie's room. The only two men Carla had slept with now faced each other. It was weird, but strangely satisfying, like giving Richard a taste of his own medicine.

"Fine. Just give me a minute," said Carla.

Michael nodded and walked back towards Jenny and Nathan who pretended to be caught up in conversation. Ignoring a derisive snort from Richard, Carla led him to a corner of the stage.

"Over here. What do you want?" she asked, determined to stay coolheaded.

"Carla, since we split up, nothing seems to/ ..."

"You mean since I caught you shagging in our bed." Carla glared at him. Typical lawyer. Put in a grain of truth and rewrite history.

"Yes. I was stupid. I admit it."

"I hope you feel better for getting it off your chest. I have a party to get back to."

As Carla stepped away, Richard caught her arm.

"Please, just hear me out."

Michael looked over. It was beginning to feel like a very long minute. Richard had his hands on Carla's shoulders and looked directly into her eyes. It was obvious that these two people had once been close. Maybe they still were. Before he realised what he was doing, Michael put his beer bottle on the bar and made his excuses. Nathan and Jenny looked at each other, and then at Carla.

In the corner of the stage Richard continued his charm offensive.

"… and now Donald has started promoting these young guns over me. I can't leave the company. I'm forty-six. It's taken years to get this far."

"How awful for you."

Carla had no idea why Richard was telling her this.

"Donald's always had a soft spot for you Carla. He keeps asking after you."

"I though it was Chlamydia he had a soft spot for. Silly me. It was a hard spot."

"Camilla, she's a nightmare. She moves from one mad project to another. She's costing me a fortune."

"Yes, it's painful to watch the family silver being stolen from under your nose."

"Carla, we could put a stop to it all, right now."

"We?" Carla stared at Richard. *What on earth is he jabbering on about?*

Richard took Carla's hands and looked straight into her eyes.

"We were a great team, Carla. We could still be. You know what I mean, get back together put everything back as it was."

Carla felt as though she'd been plunged under water. She could not longer hear the chatter around her. Sounds were low and distorted. The world was in slow motion.

"What?"

Richard gripped both her hands. Jenny nudged Nathan as they tried to read the scene unfolding in the corner of the stage.

"Just think," said Richard stepping closer to Carla. "We could buy our old house back. I know how much you loved that house."

"And you made me sell it," said Carla, a lump forming in her throat.

"I'll get it back. We can be a proper family again."

Richard's breath was warm against Carla's cold forehead. His features became blurry. She blinked hard.

"Why are you doing this?"

A tear had slipped down her cheek. Richard smoothed it away with his thumb.

"I'm lost without you. I don't know who I am anymore."

The *Match of the Day* ring tone erupted from Richard's jacket pocket.

"Sorry," he said fishing inside his jacket. "Might be a client."

Richard stepped away from Carla.

"No, you're not interrupting anything. Go ahead."

Carla glanced towards the crowded bar. The sound of chattering and laughter became sharper as her senses slipped back into real time. She looked at Richard who winked at her, phone to his ear. He was acting as if the last couple of years hadn't happened. Carla took the phone from him.

"Actually, you are interrupting something. Your lawyer is in the middle of very delicate negotiations to win back his ex wife. So, I'm going to have to ask you very nicely, to fuck off."

To Carla's surprise Richard laughed as she switched off the phone and dropped it into his open hand.

"Is that a yes?"

"On one condition," said Carla seriously.

"Anything." Richard took her hand.

"We try for another baby. What do they call it? Sticking plaster baby," said Carla with a gleam in her eye.

"Do you think that's a good idea?" he choked. "You know, at your age."

Carla burst out laughing. Same old Richard. Twisting the truth to suit him.

"I know about the vasectomy."

Richard looked relieved, oblivious that Carla had caught him lying.

"Tell me, how did you get in here?" asked Carla.

Richard looked puzzled.

"Through the door."

"When?"

"About ten minutes ago."

The penny dropped. Like a black widow spider, Carla had led the unsuspecting male into her trap. Richard felt he was about to be eaten alive.

"I mean't to come and watch the play. I was delayed," he said, sounding almost sincere.

"And what was the name of this play that you meant to come and see?"

"Well, I wasn't coming to see the play *to see the play*. I was coming to support you," said Richard smoothly.

The old Carla would have bought it. He wasn't so sure about the woman standing in front of him.

"Fuck off Richard," said Carla, angry with herself for allowing him in ten short minutes to push her back emotionally to a place she had promised herself never to return.

"Come on Carla, we're meant to be together, till death us do part."

"That can be arranged," came a voice at the end of a rifle.

Patricia pointed the barrel at Richard's chest.

"Christ, not you again."

"You heard her," said Patricia. "Fuck off."

She brought the barrel in closer.

"Alright, I'm leaving," said Richard putting his hands up. "Just think about it, Carla." He kissed her cheek.

"Bloody menopausal women," Richard muttered walking away "Not safe to be let out onto the streets."

Carla looked at Patricia in disbelief. A few people were looking and whispering in their direction.

"What?" asked Patricia. "It's just a prop I found in the cupboard."

Patricia aimed the barrel at the ceiling and pulled the trigger. A deafening shot rang out. The drinkers hit the deck splashing beer and wine everywhere. Carla looked into the auditorium. The two people who held her fate in their hands peered over the tops of their seat, eyes wide with fear. Their note pads and pens were scattered down the central isle. Carla felt like she'd been shot.

*****

That weekend was the most miserable since Carla had kicked Richard out. Her future felt grim. Michael's mobile was switched off. She wanted to talk to him, explain. She didn't blame him for walking out of the theatre. She had given Richard for more time than he deserved. If the shoe had been on the other foot she would have done the same.

Monday morning she found a note on his office door saying he would be away till the end of the week.

"He's gone to Dublin," said Jenny tucking into the chocolate fudge brownie and ice cream they were sharing in the refectory. "Flew over on Saturday. Nathan told me."

"Did he say why?" said Carla spooning a large piece of brownie into her mouth.

Her chocolate cravings had come back with a vengeance.

"Family something or other." Jenny devoured a huge blob of vanilla icecream. "God this is good."

"So good, we're having another," said Carla picking up her purse.

Over the next few days Carla ate a lot of chocolate. If Michael didn't get back soon she'd explode. Friday, and still no sign of him. She had got to Uni early and decided to walk around the lake, otherwise it would have been straight to the refectory. The sun had dispersed the early morning mist with the promise of a beautiful day. The birds made a racquet in the trees, and the sheep in the field on the far side bleated at regular intervals. She stared at the glassy surface of the lake and tried to block everything out. She wanted silence, from everything, especially from trying to guess what was going on in Michael's head. She should know by now it was useless trying to figure out what a man was thinking. Twenty years with Richard had shown her that. Closing her eyes she took in a deep breath and slowly exhaled. Tuning in to the sound of her breathing, the sounds around her began to fade.

"Hello Carla."

Carla flinched.

"I didn't mean to startle you," said Michael.

He looked tired. Carla wondered whether he'd had as many sleepless nights as her.

"You're back. Of course you are you're here. How was Ireland? Jenny told me. Nathan told her" she gabbled, afraid that if she stopped talking Michael might disappear again.

"Family crisis. You know how it is," said Michael as Carla took another breath.

"Is everything okay?" asked Carla not wanting to pry.

"I think so. We'll see."

There was an awkward silence. The night of the play hung between them. They both started talking at once.

"The other night, after the play, I hope you didn't ..." began Carla.

"Carla, if you want to ..."

Silence. Carla smiled uneasily.

"You first," she offered.

Carla looked straight into Michael's eyes. Under his knitted brows they looked serious. Her heart sank.

"All I want to say is, if you want to finish it between us, I'll understand."

"Do you want me to finish it?" asked Carla, preparing herself for the body blow.

"No, I don't," said Michael putting his hand on Carla's shoulder. "But you don't have to tell me how important family is, I'm Irish. I know. When I saw you talking with your ex-husband I saw ..."

"What you saw was Richard playing dirty," said Carla putting her hand on Michael's. "He's a lawyer. That makes him an expert. All I ever wanted was a family, loving husband, a couple of children, a nice life. I was stupid enough to think I had it."

"So you don't want to get back with him?" asked Michael unknitting his brows, a smile creeping into his soft brown eyes.

"No. I don't want Richard, only the idea of what I wanted him to be. He's too selfish to be any of those things."

Carla looked straight into Michael's eyes.

"You've already done more for me than Richard did in a life time."

Wrapped in Michael's arms Carla closed her eyes. To be with the man she trusted, someone who encouraged her to find her talents, that was more than enough. Michael was more than enough.

*****

137

Chapter Eight

The grassy slope in Victoria Park was littered with groups of people enjoying the strong June sunshine. Carla lay on her back with her white cotton cardigan over her face. Jenny lay next to her on her stomach, flicking through a file. Where the time had gone? All essays had been handed in. Just one exam and that was it. Three of the best and worst years of her life. Over. *How could so much happen in such a short space of time?*

"Ah ha," announced Jenny finding something that interested her. Name two of the all-female cabaret style theatre groups formed in the late nineteen seventies."

"Easy peasy. Clapperclaw Beryl and the Perils, and Cunning Stunts."

"Careful writing that down in the exam," chortled Jenny. "You don't want the examiner thinking you're offering favours for honours. Oh, silly me, I forgot, you're already sleeping with one of them."

Rolling onto her stomach, Carla gave Jenny a playful shove. She pulled the file of notes towards her and turned the page.

"I can't afford for anything to go wrong in these exams. I've already blown the theatre job," said Carla cringing at the memory of Patricia's grand finale to her directorial debut.

"You don't know that for sure. How is your bodyguard?"

"Patricia's mortified. She's practically adopted Robbie so I can get on and study."

A distorted rendition of a nursery rhyme cut through the sound of children squealing.

"All this studying is making me hungry." Said Jenny standing up. "Time for a very large ice-cream." She pulled Carla up by the arm. "With some sticky strawberry sauce."

"I fancy a 99" said Carla as she picked up the file and the books scattered on the grass.

"That figures," Jenny chuckled. "How are things with the Irish charmer?"

"A bit quiet since he got back," replied Carla distractedly, deciding whether to have one flake or two. With just a snatched apple for breakfast three hours earlier, her stomach was gurgling loudly.

A disorganised queue had formed around the brightly decorated van.

"Probably too much going on back in Dublin. You know what men are like. Hopeless multi-taskers-Shit!"

"That's a bit harsh," laughed Carla.

Jenny froze. She stared ahead. Following her gaze, Carla saw a familiar figure in a very unfamiliar situation. Michael was pushing a buggy. The buggy held a toddler, a little boy, an unmistakeable mini-me. Next to him strolled an attractive thirty something. They were completely wrapped up in conversation. Michael put his arm around the woman's shoulder and kissed her tenderly on the forehead. Carla and Jenny look at each other in disbelief, and looked again at the couple to make sure their eyes hadn't deceived them. Michael caught sight of them. Carla registered the look of surprise on his face. Her breath quickened, her heart pounded and the colour drained from her face. The books fell from her hands.

"How could you?" she screamed, sprinting towards him. Alarmed, Michael handed the buggy to the woman.

"Carla?" he ventured, unsure how she would manage to stop from warp speed.

In an effort avoid being winded, Michael side-stepped her. Too late. The body blow caught his left side. Arms flailing like windmills, Michael tried to stay upright, but he was already tumbling backwards.

"I'm so sorry," Carla looked at the bewildered woman apologetically. " I didn't know."

As Carla ran off down the path, Jenny snatched her books up from the ground.

"You shit," she hissed, at the figure sat spluttering in the middle of the duck pond.

One of the dozen or so scattered ducks flew in low over Michael and released a sticky white deposit. It dropped, grazing Michael's nose and landed with a splat on the front of his shirt. The toddler clapped his hands and chuckled appreciatively.

"Get that down you. You're still shaking," said Jenny handing Carla a large mug. Carla took a sip of tea. Her eyes were red rimmed and glazed with shock as she stared blankly around her kitchen. The cheerful yellow walls mocked her. Happiness was just a trick of the light.

"I can't believe, how I could have been so stupid." Carla shook her head willing the images of Michael's family, playing over in her head, to switch off.

"It's not your fault. He had me fooled. All that crap about visiting his parents. He's the bloody parent." Jenny saw Carla's face crumple and put her arms around her friend.

"Lying toe rag." Carla laid her head on Jenny's shoulder releasing deep, painful sobs.

From inside her handbag, Carla's ringtone, Puccini's Un Bel Di Vedremo filled the room. Carla cried harder.

The next morning Jenny marched into the lecture theatre. Michael stood at the lectern sorting his papers. Class wasn't due to start for another ten minutes and his students weren't the best timekeepers, so he glanced to wards the door. He was both annoyed and concerned to see Jenny goose stepping towards him.

"Where's Carla? She's not answering my calls," he asked, sounding a more aggressive than intended. It was nearing the end of term and he was feeling more frayed around the edges than usual.

"And you're surprised? God, that's rich." Hands on hips Jenny was pumped and ready for a fight.

"Has she lost the plot?"

Jenny snorted. "For getting upset over your little secret?"

"Nula?"

Waving an arm around for dramatic effect, Jenny replied, "Nula, Carla. Easy to mix them up."

"Nula and Marius are my family," said Michael firmly.

"Ah, so you admit it," cut in Jenny savouring her Miss Marple moment.

"Of course I admit it. She's my sister for God's sake." Tired and wound up, it was Michael's turn to take the high ground.

"S-sister?" Jenny's eyebrows drew towards the bridge of her nose as she processed the information.

"Not that it's any of your business," he said pointedly, "Nula has been having some relationship problems, so I invited her to Bath for a few days. She needed time to think, before doing something she might later regret."

The sarcasm passed over Jenny's head. The aggressive stance had been replace by an embarrassed shuffle.

"Oh dear."

"I didn't want to bother Carla. She has enough of her plate right now, but ..." Michael paused, "if she can't trust me then maybe we shouldn't be together."

Jenny defended her friend. "Maybe you shouldn't expect everything to be perfect."

The words hung in the air. Both of them had a feeling they were not alone. They turned cautiously to face the main door and saw that the room was full of students listening intently Some were taking notes. With an awkward smile,

Jenny slid into a seat in the front row. Michael stood behind the lectern and cleared his throat.

"Thank you for that demonstration Jenny. A highly competent piece of acting.

Jenny nodded earnestly, hoping the students would buy into the charade.

"As you have just experienced," continued Michael, settling into his performance, "today we are examining Augusto Boal's Invisible Theatre. Now, how many of you believed that conversation was real?"

All the hands shot up. Michael surveyed his audience with exaggerated satisfaction.

"Excellent. Excellent."

*****

Jenny emptied the soup carton into a saucepan.

"Carrot and coriander okay?"

"Fine," shrugged Carla, sawing through a bloomer like a piece of wood. "I've blown it, haven't I?"

Jenny stirred the soup.

"I'm sure you haven't." She wasn't entirely convincing.

"He thinks I'm a mad cow." Carla's sawing intensified.

"He's a good man. He'll come round."

Jenny stirred faster. Three days of Carla wallowing in a pit of self-pity was wearing thin.

"Come round to thinking he's had a lucky escape." Carla stabbed the bloomer.

Jenny stopped stirring.

"Carla, it will work itself out."

"You don't know that," said Carla petulantly.

Jenny slammed the spoon on the counter.

"You know what Carla? It will work itself out, simply because, you are one of those people who falls in shit and comes out smelling of roses.

The tip of the knife jabbed Carla's thumb.

"Ouch!" Carla put her thumb in her mouth and sucked. "Wassa susposta mean?"

"It means you have a wonderful family, a man who adores you, and the prospect of a great job."

It was too late to grab the pan. The soup boiled over, hissing as it hit the hob.

"Shit!" Jenny switched off the gas. "Even your ex husband wants you back, and you're still complaining."

Jenny tore off handfuls of kitchen roll, screwed it up and pressed it into the spillage.

"Nobody's looked at me since Martin died."

Carla took her thumb out of her mouth.

"I didn't think you wanted anyone else."

Jenny slopped the remainder of the soup into two bowls.

"Everyone wants to be loved Carla. We all need to be loved."

"If you started by loving yourself then/"

"What?" replied Jenny, stung.

Carla had hit nerve and she continued drilling.

"If you didn't spent your life in a drunken haze, maybe somebody *would* love you."

"Meaning?"

Jenny knew this conversation had slipped over a precipice. She didn't care. If Carla had something to say, make her spell it out. Carla pointed at the dozen or so empty wine bottles next to the bin.

"Says it all."

With their friendship heading towards a crash landing, Jenny wanted to get the inevitable over with.

"I need a drink to cope with listening to you whining on about your non-existent problems."

Jenny threw the saucepan into the sink. Crash!

Carla picked up her bag.

"Really. Well, don't worry I won't bother you with them again."

She picked up a slice of bread, ripped a mouthful out of it and flounced out. Slam! Jenny slumped into a chair, and stared at the table. Two bowls looked back at her like a pair of watery eyes.

Surrounded by textbooks crammed on the kitchen table, Carla struggled to organise her thoughts. Although determined to push the fight with Jenny to the back of her mind, it refused to stay there. Carla's stomach gurgled, reminding her it had been two hours since she had shoved that slice of bread into her mouth.

Apart from half a carton of tomato and basil soup, the fridge was empty. She poured the contents into a pan and stirred. Maybe Jenny had a point. Yes, she had fallen in the shit, but Michael had been waiting, it seemed, to pick her up and then to love her. Steam rose from the bowl. Carla lifted the spoon to her lips. Who had been there for Jenny through long lonely evenings? Dropping the spoon in the bowl, Carla reached into her bag and pulled out her phone.

I must be otherwise engaged so leave a message-chirped Jenny. Carla threw the phone back in her bag and grabbed her keys.

Carla walked briskly to Jenny's front door. Eating humble pie was not one of her fortes, but she owed Jenny that much. The doorbell rang sharply inside the house. No answer. Carla held her finger on the button. Still no answer. She peered through the letterbox. Jenny's bag was on the floor in the hallway. Music played in the sitting room.

"Jen, it's me," called Carla through the letterbox. "Please, open the door."

Jenny's tabby, Winston, appeared in the hallway. He made his way to the front door and meowed at the eyes the other side of the letterbox.

"Come on Jen," urged Carla. "I know you're in there."

"Meow." Winston stared at the letterbox.

Carla's stomach was doing somersaults. She ran to the back of the house. She spotted a wooden door leading into Jenny's garden, and tugged at the latch. It was bolted from inside.

"Bugger!"

Carla scanned the lane. There was a metal bin a couple of houses along. She dragged the bin to the back gate, gingerly placed a foot on the lid and gripped the top of the gate. Hoisting herself up, Carla swung her legs over, and attempted to jump clear of the gate.

"Ow!"

She landed heavily on one side and felt a sharp pull on her right ankle.

"When I get my hands on you Jenny Longmore, " muttered Carla, trying to rub away the pain, "you're a dead woman."

Carla hobbled up the garden path and rattled the back door handle. Locked. The kitchen window was barely open, and secured with and old-fashioned catch. Winston trotted into the kitchen as Carla peered in through the window. He looked straight at her and resumed his pitiful meowing. Carla tried to force her hand through the gap in the window to release the catch, but only succeeded in scrapping her knuckles. She looked around Jenny's neatly arranged garden. Tall sticks supported sweet peas. Just the job. Carla drew one out and held it up.

"Ah ha, I won't be defeated that easily."

She hobbled back to the window, slipped the cane under the catch and released it.

"Aargh!" Carla heaved herself up, stepped onto the kitchen counter, and tried to avoid slipping into the sink. She slid off the counter landing on the hard floor.

" Bugger, bugger, bugger, bugger!"

Her ankle throbbed harder.

"Meow," replied Winston into the hall towards the music.

Charlene Spiteri belted out that she didn't need a lover.

"Jen? Where are you?"

As Carla followed Winston towards the living room she felt increasingly unnerved. She pushed the door slowly open. On the mantelpiece behind four lit tea lights, a younger, unwounded Jenny, her head on Martin's shoulder, looked back at her.

"Jen, are you there?"

Carla stepped hesitantly into the room, her blood pounding against her eardrums. The sofa was behind the door. Jenny was sprawled on it face down. Her arm dangled on the floor. An empty whiskey bottle lay close by.

"Shit!"

Carla gripped Jenny by the shoulders, turned her and tried to shake her conscious.

"Wake up. Come on. Wake up!"

The limp body failed to respond. Hands trembling, Carla punched at her phone.

"I need an ambulance. Quick. My friend is unconscious."

Twenty minutes later, paramedics carried Jenny out on a stretcher. Carla closed the front door. She noticed a growing group of neighbours looking on with a mixture of curiosity and concern.

"Are you sure there was no sign of any other substances?" asked a female paramedic.

Carla thought she didn't look much older than Isabella.

"Yes, quite sure. Can I go with her?"

"Of course."

Carla climbed into the ambulance, trying to ignore the increasing throb in her ankle.

The nurse finished strapping Carla's ankle.

"There you are. A couple of weeks and you'll be fine. Just try and keep the weight off it."

"Thank you. Can I see my friend now?"

Carla wondered what kind of reception she would get, but vowed to take anything Jenny threw at her. She had been a rotten friend, wrapped up in her insignificant problems, oblivious to Jenny's torment.

"Follow me." The nurse led Carla down a long corridor and into a small room. Jenny's eyes were closed, but she was no longer lifeless

"Thanks." Carla hoped the nurse didn't sense her guilt.

Jenny's hand felt reassuringly warm. Her eyelids flickered, then, slowly opened.

"I'm so sorry Jen, I feel awful."

"Don't flatter yourself Bianco, I'm not that fond of you."

Carla laughed, relieved. They were friends again. Stroking Jenny's hand, Carla had to ask. Such a drastic step was alien to her. Even at her lowest, her determination to make sure Isabella and Robbie were fine, overrode all other emotions.

"Why Jen?"

"I just wanted to take away the pain ... of not having Martin. Without him the future feels like a black hole."

"Some things take a long time to adjust to. There are bound to be setbacks. And none of us know what the future holds. Today Jen, that's all we have."

"Actually, we have an exam *tomorrow*."

"Alright smart arse. So, let's take it a step at a time. Step one. Get the exam out of the way," said Carla.

They were going to graduate together. No argument.

"Oh God," moaned Jenny.

"God helps those who help themselves. You need to rest. I'll be back to collect you first thing in the morning. Okay?"

"You're not going to leave me in peace unless I agree." Jenny pulled the covers over her head.

"Clever girl. I'll see you tomorrow, bright eyed and bushy tailed."

"Please. Spare the wholesome as apple pie act," groaned Jenny from under the sheet.

Carla pulled the sheet from Jenny's face and leant in.

"Listen to me you dirty, drunken bitch. Be up and ready to take that exam tomorrow or there'll be hell to pay."

Carla kissed her friend on the forehead and hobbled out with as much grace as her throbbing ankle would allow.

*****

"Damn!"

Robbie's driving game was getting the better of him. The rumble from the computer drifted into Carla's bedroom, where she sat up in bed bolstered by pillows. Books lay scattered around her, and a pile of neatly written index cards was growing on the bedside table. Tomorrow she would be able to put the books away and throw the cards in the bin. Three years at university- over. In truth, she didn't want it to end. The lectures, essays and presentations and given her structure and security when her personal life had disintegrated around her. Would she have had the courage to throw Richard out if she'd still been a full time wife? One thing she was sure of, it would only have been a matter of time before he cheated on her again. Then, along came Michael, caring, patient Michael, and she'd pushed *him* too far. After the exam she would find him and apologise. Losing Michael was not an option.

"Yes!" Robbie was triumphant."

"Time to turn that thing off," said Carla, her head around Robbie's door.

"I'm nearly on the next level." Robbie's eyes were fixed to the screen.

"Off!"

With huff, Robbie shut down the game. Drawings on Robbie's bed caught Carla's eye. She sat on the bed to take a closer look at Robbie's detailed drawings of his favourite Ferraris.

"These are really good."

Robbie sat next to Carla.

"Uncle Gianni's been helping me with my technique. I'd like to design my own cars one day."

"Put your mind to it and you will." Carla picked up the drawings and put them on Robbie's desk. "Night, night. Don't let the bedbugs bite." Carla teased her son. He may have grown half a dozen inches in the past three years but he was still her little boy.

"Night." Robbie pulled back his quilt.

As she placed her hand on the door handle, a thought occurred to Carla.

"Robbie? If anything was bothering you, you would tell me wouldn't you?"

Robbie's head nestled into the pillow.

"Well, if you must know, I'm really hacked off that Ferrari didn't win the Grand Prix.

"Good," said Carla, relieved that Ferrari's fortunes were the limit of her son's worries. "I mean, that's a shame. Maybe next year."

"Night, night. Don't let the bed bugs bite." Robbie closed his eyes.

Back in her bed, Carla picked up her pen. Ten thirty. Another hour and she'd be done. Eleven fifteen. Carla's chin rested on her chest. Pen still in hand, she snored lightly, a smile on her face as she relived her first dance with Michael at the Student's Union 80s night.

*****

"Mum! Get up. It's half eight!"

Carla forced her eyelids to separate.

"What""

"We've overslept. Get up!"

"Bugger!"

Carla leapt out of bed.

"Aargh!"

She was supine again. Okay, so rushing wasn't an option. Sitting on the bed she pulled on a T shirt and a loose cotton skirt. Index cards in hand she hobbled down the stairs. No time for breakfast. She picked up her bag, and saw Robbie's schoolbag in the hallway.

"Shit!" She'd forgotten about Robbie.

"Robbie, would you phone Patricia for a lift?" she shouted.

Already in his school uniform, Robbie appeared at the top of the stairs.

"She's on her way!"

"You star."

"Good luck mum."

"Thanks. I'm going to need it."

The hospital car park was already busy. With a lopsided hobble, Carla made her way to Jenny's room.

"Sorry I'm l-" Carla realised she was talking to an empty bed. "Bugger!"

"Looking for someone?"

Jenny stepped out of the bathroom. She put a tablet in her mouth and took a swig out of the glass in her hand.

"Thank God. Let's get going. We're late," urged Carla.

"Sshh ... bad head. It's a sign," Jenny said with a grimace. "No more alcohol."

Jenny's face was paler than usual, but Carla had no time for sympathy. She was on a mission. In a nanosecond the glass was out of Jenny's hand and she was dragged out of the room.

"Shouldn't all these people be at work, instead of jamming up the roads?" Carla's knuckles were white, her stomach in knots. This last hurdle was proving difficult to clear.

Trying to ignore her throbbing head, Jenny stared at Carla's index cards, silently mouthing the notes.

"My mouth is as dry as a monkey's armpit."

Jenny stuck her tongue out in disgust.

"You're dehydrated. There's a bottle of water in the glove compartment."

They reached the university entrance.

"Thank God," Carla exhaled.

The car bobbed over sleeping policemen and cattle grids. They finally reached the car park. And it was packed.

"Just one space. That's all I'm asking," pleaded Carla eyes to the heavens. "Give us a break."

"He's not listening." Jenny drained the water bottle.

"Right. That's it," said Carla decisively as she mounted a low grassy bank and parked on the playing field.

Jenny ran ahead of Carla's hobble. Suddenly she stopped and turned to Carla.

"Where are we going?"

"Umm …E5," replied Carla through gritted teeth.

Jenny grabbed Carla's hand and dragged her along.

"Nearly there."

Out of breath they entered the block and looked around the hall for a place to sit. They turned to each other with the same question. Who were these geeks? A middle-aged man approached them.

"Environmental Science?"

The women shook their heads.

"Theatre Studies," said Jenny almost apologetic.

"I thought so." The invigilator smiled benignly. "Try D block."

Carla felt her arm yanked out of its socket as Jenny took off again.

Worried faces already occupied most of the desks. The invigilator looked unimpressed at Carla and Jenny's tardy, bedraggled arrival. They wheezed their way to a couple of spare places and slumped into the seats. *Just as well it's the last exam* thought Carla. *I'm getting too old for this.*

151

The invigilator checked the clock. One minute to ten. Carla soothed her nerves by setting out five identical pens in a neat row. Checking her pockets and bag, Jenny realised she was penless. She looked over her shoulder and gesticulated writing movements at Carla.

"This may be a drama exam, but you will be disqualified for miming at other students," said the invigilator coldly, making Jenny's head pound harder.

"What is the problem?"

"I haven't got a pen," replied Jenny, feeling like she was back at primary school.

"What kind of student turns up at an examination without a pen?" the cold voice mocked.

"Uhh, the kind that tries to drink herself to death the day before." Jenny looked directly at the invigilator. "As you can see I failed miserably so I thought I might as well sit the exam. See if I can succeed at something."

Unsure of how to take this, the invigilator looked at Carla for a clue. Carla made a "crazy" gesture with her finger and handed the invigilator two of her pens. Avoiding eye contact with Jenny, the invigilator placed the pens on Jenny's desk. Jenny winked at Carla. A loud cough announced charades was over.

"Good luck. You may start."

Fifteen minutes in, Carla and Jenny were scribbling at a rate of knots. Michael hovered in the doorway. All he could see was the top of Carla's head and her hand moving furiously across the page. With a satisfied smile he checked his watch and returned to his office.

"Pens down please," came the command after the five minute warning. "Pens down!"

Papers collected, the hall erupted. Jenny ran over to Carla and gave her a hug.

"Brilliant notes. Thanks."

They floated into the sunshine on a wave of excited chatter about parties and celebrations, but Carla knew she had one more test to pass before she could celebrate.

"Jen, I want to find Michael. Do you mind?"

"Well, that's easy enough. He's over there," pointed Jenny.

On the opposite side of the road, briefcase in hand, Michael walked briskly in the direction of the main gates. Attempting to mask her hobble. Carla crossed the road.

"Michael, hang on!"

Michael stopped and faced her. Carla thought he looked understandably serious, but she was confident she could win him round if she grovelled hard enough.

"I did it. Last one over," she smiled tentatively, anxious for his approval.

"How did it go?"

Michael sounded natural. Carla took it as a good sign.

"Great."

Carla searched Michael's face for clues, but he wasn't giving anything away.

"Jenny told me about your sister. Nula, isn't it?"

Carla was working up to an apology.

"Yes."

"That's a nice name." It was time to plunge in. "Michael, I'm so sorry."

"For pushing me into the duck pond or for not trusting me?"

He didn't sound annoyed, just matter of fact. Carla told herself to try harder.

"Both. It's no excuse, I know, but after Richard ... people would look at me like I was a misfit, and then I saw you with Nula/-"

"Carla I/-"

"Can't we just put it behind us?"

Carla's stomach had sunk to her knees. A car slowed alongside them.

"Come on. You've got a plane to catch," chivvied Nathan.

Carla felt like she'd had a bucket of cold water thrown over her.

"Carla ..." Michael looked uncomfortable. "I've got a job interview."

"Where?"

"Dublin."

His eyes looked through her to Nathan, who honked his horn.

"I have to go."

By the time Carla had absorbed the full meaning behind their exchange the car was already outside the university grounds. Jenny was at her side and looked at Carla's ashen face.

"I heard."

With her arm around Carla, Jenny led her to the car. Carla put her head on Jenny's shoulder.

"By the way Carla. Your T shirt's on inside out."

The car park had started to empty out. It was only when they reached the car they saw it was clamped.

"Bollocks!" Carla kicked the wheel. "Aarrgh-shit!"

Pain shot through her ankle. Carla sank onto the grass and sobbed.

Two hours later, Carla's pain was numbing in direct relation to the number of shots she'd downed. Number four made her feel particularly chilled. They were at The Hope and Anchor where Michael had rescued Carla on her fortieth birthday. Now he had abandoned her too. Maybe there was something wrong with her.

"I'll 'ave another double of wharrever it was I just 'ad."

"Southern Comfort." The barman picked up a fresh glass.

"Yesshh. A double Southern Comfort to sooth my pain. My ankle is fucking killing me."

Carla's leg was propped up on a stool next to Jenny.

"Another mint tea for me please."

Jenny eyed Carla's slumped figure, and saw herself as she'd been since Martin died."

"Why didn't someone tell how tedious drunks were? I'd have quit drinking years ago," she said, only half addressing the barman.

Slowly, Carla slid. The barman grabbed her arms from across the counter. Jenny grabbed her waist.

"Cancel the drinks."

Outside, in the pub car park, June sunshine had given way to a summer tempest. Jenny had dragged Carla to the car where she lay face down on the bonnet. Fishing the keys out of Carla's bag, Jenny unlocked the passenger door. She held Carla up by her waistband and maneuvered her into the seat. The seatbelt tightened around Carla, but before Jenny had a chance to buckle her in, Carla lurched forward and wretched, emptying the contents of her stomach over Jenny's shoes.

*****

Chapter Nine

"Isabella Maria Bianco."

In cap and gown, Isabella strode beaming across the stage. Like her mother, Isabella had given up the Sterling surname. The Biancos were her family. Carla, Robbie, Patricia, Brian, and the twins clapped enthusiastically.

"Nellie Georgia Goodall."

Nellie followed in Isabella's wake. Clutching their scrolls, the young women hugged each other. Carla scanned the academics lining the stage. She did a double take at the sight of a handsome dark haired man. She felt a stab in her heart.

Two weeks had passed since Michael had flown off to Dublin. He hadn't contacted her. Carla knew from Nathan that he was spending some time at his parent's house, marking papers and catching up with old friends, before the job interview. It sounded to Carla as though he was preparing to settle back in his native country. She'd kept herself busy, and tea total. Even so, Michael was constantly in her thoughts. There was nothing she could do about that, she told herself. She would just have to be patient, and over time the longing for Michael would diminish. At least that was what she told herself.

*****

The evening sun lit up The Rondo Theatre foyer. Nathan handed Carla a large bunch of keys.

"Congratulations,"

The white haired woman shook Carla's hand.

"Thank you." Carla was grateful that Patricia's impression of Calamity Jane had been forgiven.

"You have a lot to live up to," added the thin-faced man, fellow survivor of the shooting incident.

"I do." Carla smiled at Nathan. "The theatre will have my undivided attention."

They left Nathan to brief Carla. She heaved a sigh of relief.

"Thanks Nathan."

"What for?"

"For believing in me."

She kissed him on the cheek.

"You believed in yourself. The theatre is all yours."

"That's a scary thought. Doing this all on my own."

"You're not. I'm here for you. Whenever you need me." Nathan kissed Carla on the cheek. "Good luck."

Nathan walked towards the door, then, looked back at Carla.

"Do you think Jenny might be free tonight?" he asked hesitantly.

"Take a chance. Give her a call."

"I think I will."

Alone in the dark auditorium, Carla relived her directorial debut. In the shadows she felt Michael's presence, next to her, squeezing her hand, as strongly as if he was actually there. But he wasn't.

*****

The capping and gowning process was running like a well-oiled machine. The hall was packed with caped crusaders.

"These gowns weigh a ton," puffed Jenny.

"We'll melt in this heat." Carla tried on a cap that perched precariously on her head.

"Too small!" Jenny picked up a cap. "I could do with melting away a few pounds. "University may be good for the brain but it's very bad for the arse." Jenny disappeared under her cap.

"Too big!" Carla picked up another cap.

"Just right!" they chorused.

"So, has he been in touch?" Jenny hadn't asked about Michael some time.

"No." Carla's voice cracked beneath her forced smile.

"Then fuck him!" announced Jenny. "If the great Dr Nolan is a prick, fuck him. You're not a student any more. You're free to shag your way through the whole faculty."

The chatter around them dimmed. Eyes cast sideways in Carla's direction.

"Thanks Jenny, I think everyone has got the picture," whispered Carla through gritted teeth. Bringing her cap

157

down over her eyes, Carla sidled towards the door. Following her, Jenny looked over her shoulder at the whispering huddles.

"Just kidding!"

A large marque had been erected on the green lawn overlooked by the old manor house. It was the turn of the drama students to collect their degrees. Mamma Bianco, Isabella, and Robbie watched Carla waiting at one side of the stage. Carla took a deep breath.

"Carla Bianco."

Carla stepped forward and smiled at the audience. The voice continued.

"Living proof that eighty per cent of female students will sleep with their lecturers to get a First."

A gasp from the audience. Mamma Bianco crossed herself. Frozen on the spot, Carla wanted the ground to swallow her up.

"Carla Annunziata Pompea Bianco."

Unaccustomed to hearing her name in all its glory, Carla was jolted out of her daydream.

Isabella and Robbie looked at each other. Their mother had kept that quiet. Their shoulders shook with supressed laughter. Mamma slapped them both across the head. She clapped proudly as Carla received her scroll.

"My daughter," she said loudly, poking the woman in front of her.

"Get ready. One. Two. Three."

Two caps flew up. Click. Isabella captured the end of Carla's and Jenny's three year adventure.

*****

University College Dublin was unusually quiet. The students had deserted the campus for the summer. Michael sat on a plastic chair. He had felt subdued since leaving

Bath, but put it down to nerves. He told himself that there was a reason this job had come up now. It was time to go home.

"We're ready to see you now Michael."

Patrick McGuiness, a silver haired man close to retirement showed Michael into the interview room. He indicated a chair to Michael and took a seat next to his colleague, an attractive red head in her forties. She immediately put on her glasses to get a better look at Michael.

"You have a very impressive CV," she purred.

"So," added Patrick, "tell us what you are looking to get from this position?"

Michael was on autopilot.

"A new challenge."

Katrina crossed her legs seductively revealing the inside of her thigh.

"And you expect to find that here?"

She kicked off her shoe and ran a foot up her leg. She wouldn't mind giving Michael a few challenges. It had been five years since her last challenge, and he'd buggered off to become head of department in some obscure university in Wales.

Michael's hesitation filled with memories of Carla; the iced tea encounter, their first dance, the hot air balloon incident, and the defeated look on her face as he drove off to catch his plane.

"Michael? Do you believe you will find that here?" repeated Katrina.

Michael was up on his feet.

"No. I mean … sorry, I have to go."

Patrick scratched his head. Katrina pulled of her glasses. A record departure. Where was she going wrong?

*****

159

Bianco's Mangia Bene was lit up like a Christmas tree for the graduation celebrations. Gianni's artwork lined a wall ready for the tourists to take home a little bit of England. Mamma Bianco, Nina and Gina came to the end of a rousing rendition of My Way. A storm of applause followed. Carla took the microphone and waited a few moments for the cheers to die down.

"I'm not going to inflict my singing on you. Mamma's the one with the voice."

More cheers.

"I just wanted to say thank you to everyone who has helped me to get to this moment. To my amazing family … "

Carla paused. Applause.

" … and to my wonderful, if slightly mad friends, Patricia, Jenny, Nathan and …"

Carla raised her glass. Jenny looked a Nathan. Michael's name hung silently in the air."

"Everyone," continued Carla. "Right," she waved the microphone, "next contender for The X Factor?"

Nellie grabbed the mic and gestured to Isabella to join her. Carla made her way to Jenny and Nathan.

"You okay?" ventured Jenny.

"Great."

All three winced. Behind them Isabella and Nellie murdered Somewhere Over The Rainbow.

"Time to mingle."

Carla picked up a tray of mini pizzas from the counter and approached a large group by the door. Patricia's hand hovered over the tray with indecision.

"They look delicious."

A cool breeze blew in from the door. Michael paused in the doorway and scanned the room. The tray wobbled.

"Let me take that from you."

Patricia slid the tray out of Carla's hand. Michael faced Carla.

"What are you doing here? I-I thought you were in Ireland."

The protective shell that Carla had built around herself started to crack.

"I was."

Michael appeared calm. Carla's heart felt like lead.

"And?"

"I'm not taking the job."

Carla waited for more. The group around her chomped nervously on pizza. Brian went in for the last piece. Patricia slapped his hand, picked it up and ripped a chunk out of it with her teeth.

"I want us to be together," said Michael simply.

"Until when Michael? Until the next time I something irrationally rational."

Carla's heart had been stamped on enough. If she put herself in a position for it to happen again she only had herself to blame.

"I didn't get the job/-"

"So I'm the booby prize," cut in Carla. The sooner this was over, the sooner she could get on with her life.

"I walked out of the interview."

A tentative "aah" arose from the women close enough to eavesdrop. The rest of the guests were having their eardrums shredded by Nellie and Isabella belting out an unrecognisable rendition of I Will Always Love You.

"So, you decided to walk out of the interview and stroll back into my life." Carla's eyes flashed with anger. Anger was less painful than feeling desolate.

Michael put his hands on Carla's shoulders.

"Please. Don't move."

He walked towards Isabella and Nellie as they built up to the final chorus.

"Do you mind?" Michael put his hand out for the mic. Nellie slammed the mic onto his palm.

"We're not that bad," she said indignantly.

The backing track reached its climactic final chorus as Michael put the mic to his mouth.

"Carla Bianco," he burred.

All eyes were fixed on Michael.

"Ti amo. I love you."

All heads swivelled towards Carla. A tear breached the protective shell and ran down her cheek.

"Please come to Ireland this weekend and meet my family. My sister, in particular, would like to get to know you better."

In spite of herself, Carla laughed.

"Musta be serious," said Nina to Mamma Bianco. "Ees learnin' Italain.

"Gotta a gooda job too," added Mamma Bianco, "ees a plumber.

Nina and Gina nodded approvingly. Gina clasped her hand to her chest.

"Ee looks so 'andsome."

"Like my Enzo."

Mamma Bianco blew loudly into her handkerchief. The three women crossed themselves.

A tear rolled down Carla's cheek as she looked into Michael's hopeful face.

"Is that a yes?" asked Michael, hoping he'd made enough of a spectacle of himself to win Carla over.

Too choked to speak, Carla nodded. The guests burst into spontaneous applause. Isabella ran through the karaoke list and clicked. Brown Eyed Girl, cueing Michael to take Carla in his arms.

"I love you too," whispered Carla.

Michael cupped her face in his hands and kissed her. Around them the guests filled the dance floor. Isabella and Nellie picked up the microphone and launched into the catchy chorus.

*****

It was the start of the winter season at The Rondo Theatre. The final moments of Educating Rita were playing out on stage.

Laura, playing Rita, raised her scissors to cut the professor's hair. Carla looked proudly on at Michael in his role as Frank. Rita snipped close to the professor's ear.

"Ouch!"

Blackout. The lights came up to a burst of applause from an audience full of family and friends. The cast took a bow, and called Carla up to join them. Quentin clapped magnanimously.

"I trained her you know," he said to the woman next to him.

A heavily pregnant Jenny presented Carla and Laura with flowers. She took her seat next to Nathan. Jenny placed his hand on the top of her bump. Their baby kicked against his palm.

Still drinking in the applause, Michael squeezed Carla's left hand, running his thumb over the platinum wedding ring he had placed on his wife's finger the month before. Carla smiled at her husband. A flick of a switch in the lighting box filled the stage with a warm glow. Happiness, thought Carla, was more than just a trick of the light.

*****

THE END

Made in the USA
Charleston, SC
21 July 2014